INHERITED MALICE

A DARK SECRET SOCIETY ROMANCE

ALTA HENSLEY
STASIA BLACK

Special Thank you to our editor, Maggie Ryan, and our wonderful beta readers.

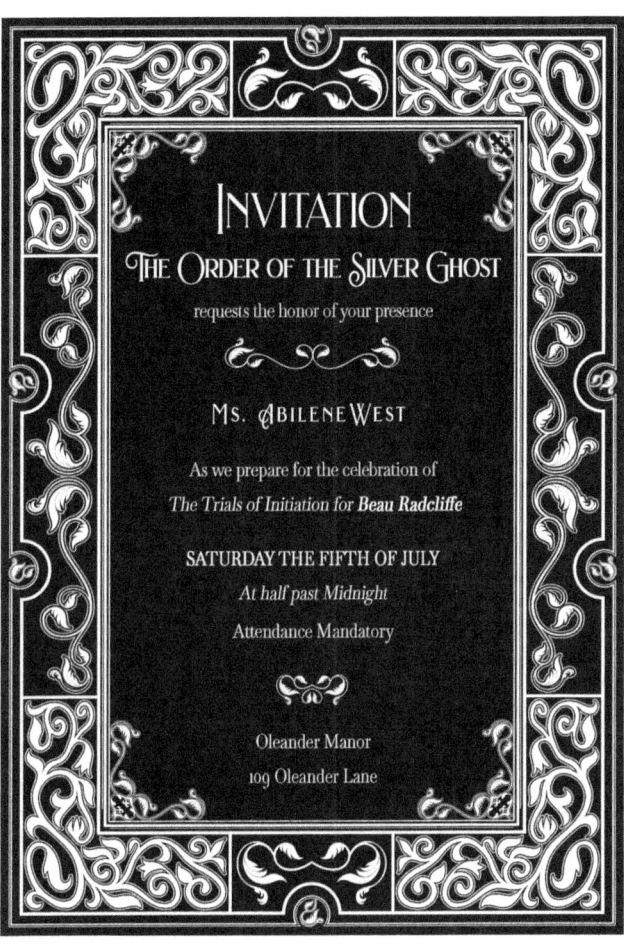

INVITATION

THE ORDER OF THE SILVER GHOST

requests the honor of your presence

MS. ABILENE WEST

As we prepare for the celebration of

The Trials of Initiation for **Beau Radcliffe**

SATURDAY THE FIFTH OF JULY

At half past Midnight

Attendance Mandatory

Oleander Manor

109 Oleander Lane

1

CONSUELA

I watched carefully as the man in full ostentatious livery walked into the bar in the tiny Georgia town. I'd beaten him into the bar by a full thirty seconds, and my heart still raced a mile a minute.

I'd hoped for time to be able to order a drink and look more natural, but the bartender was flirting with some chick at the other end of the bar. I'd dressed intentionally inconspicuously. After all, I was trying to blend in.

It wasn't the bartender's attention I was after tonight. No, I'd have to play this *verrrry* carefully if I didn't want to fuck it up royally. I had one shot.

I'd pray if I was the praying sort. But no, I remembered Tina's words from the foster home as she taught me the tricks of the trade.

I didn't have to have luck—or God—on my side.

I didn't even have to be the smartest person in the room.

I just had to be the wiliest. I had to be the one analyzing every angle, every person. Looking for the marks, for the weak links, for the *ins* and the levers I could pull to manipulate people to get them to do exactly what I wanted.

I wasn't as good as Tina.

No one was as good as Tina. She'd taught me everything she knew, used me for one last con and then spit me out when I wasn't useful to her.

Like I said, she taught me everything I knew.

I pulled out my phone and pretended to be absorbed in the small screen while surreptitiously watching out the corner of my eye as the old dude in the tux with tails presented the beautiful girl in the corner with the calligraphed invitation.

She looked confused, but then recognition dawned in her eyes. Shit. She knew what it meant. I wouldn't go so far as to pry the invitation out of her cold, dead hands or anything, but I was walking out of here with it, one way or the other. She just didn't know it yet.

Old Man Tuxedo finally exited out the way he'd come and the woman in the corner ordered another round of drinks from a passing waitress. But then she paused, pulled out her wallet, and sent the waitress on her way without ordering anything after all.

Aha. It was just like I'd heard. The Order really did prey on women who had no other choices. Fucking bastards.

I smiled.

Because what made this woman a perfect mark for the Order also made her perfect for me.

Time to go in for the kill. So to speak.

I grabbed my purse and headed straight for the woman's table.

"Is this seat taken?" I asked, pointing at the chair across from her where she sat at the small square table.

The woman looked up, confused at my sudden appearance.

I sat down before she could say one way or the other. I called over the waitress who had just passed by. "Drinks are on me. What are you having?"

That perked her up a little. "Vodka and coke."

I smiled. "Classic. Two vodka and cokes."

The waitress nodded without much interest and walked off.

"Hi, I'm Vanessa," I said, holding out a hand across the table. Lie. My name was actually Connie, but I hadn't used that name since the group home. I'd been running one grift or another since then, and any idiot knew you didn't use a name that could be traced back.

The invitation lay glittering right there on the tabletop between us, but I held my gaze right on the pretty woman's face, not once even glancing down.

Hesitantly, she lifted her hand and shook mine. "Uh, hi. Abilene. But I go by Abby."

I grinned at her. "Hi, Abby. I'm new in town, but I grew up just one county over. You know Burrows Creek?"

She smiled and her posture relaxed a little. "Sure. I think we played y'all in football."

I laughed at that. "Where'd you go?"

"Simmons High."

"Oh damn, y'all creamed us every time."

She laughed. "We almost went to state my senior year. We creamed everybody."

Restlessly, she fingered the invitation on the table.

This was almost too easy.

The waitress brought our drinks back, and I pretended to sip mine while encouraging Abby to order another—on me, naturally.

She tried to protest but I waved it away. "It's the end of a long week and it's nice to meet someone new in town. I've been down on my luck, and I'll take *any* friendly face at this point."

Her face grew immediately sympathetic. "Oh my God, I know exactly what you mean! My ex just kicked me out—apparently, he's been hooking up with some bitch from the nail salon who's barely out of high school. I went down there and confronted her about moving in on my man, and then her boss called *my* boss at the strip mall one street over cause they knew each other, and I lost *my* job. This town fucking sucks."

Then she looked up at me. "Sorry. Like, I know you just moved here and all. But I can't wait to get the hell out of here."

I nodded sympathetically as she started picking at the corner of the invitation on the table again. "What's that?" I asked, as innocently as I could muster.

She scoffed. "Crazy. Crazy is what this is." She shook her head and picked up the gold-inscribed invitation.

Then she laid it down again and covered it up with her hand, glancing around her like she might get caught doing something by someone watching her.

She leaned in over the table, and I leaned in too.

"You grew up around here, right?"

I nodded.

"So have you ever heard of the Order? Like, that secret society thing that can offer pretty girls anything they ever wanted and make all their dreams come true?"

I licked my lips and then cursed myself for giving away such a tell. I tried to be more nonchalant as I nodded and then paused, my eyes going to the Invitation.

"Wait. You aren't saying—" I scoffed and pretended to swig some of my drink, not really letting any of the actual liquid into my mouth.

Then I leaned in further and lowered my voice to a whisper. "I mean I saw that weird guy come in here. You aren't saying that's it? One of the, like, Invitation things?"

Her eyes got wide, and she nodded.

"Shut the front door!" I yelped and slapped the table.

She giggled and waved her hands at me, shushing. "Shhhh." She looked around us again. "Shhh, I don't want anyone else to know."

I nodded and pretended to zip my lips closed. I moved around the table to a seat that was closer to her and then asked, "But seriously, are you just fucking with me? No way that guy actually gave you one of those Invitations. I thought it was all just made up."

"It's not! Look!"

She handed me the Invitation. Just *handed* it to me.

I took the precious, crisp thick-stock paper in my hand and carefully skimmed the gold lettering.

The Trials of Initiation for Beau Radcliffe.

Oh shit. There it was in black and white.

His name.

Beau Radcliffe.

I hadn't even known his last name for the longest time. When I first heard his first name, I laughed. I thought it was bow like *bowtie*, and I wondered who would ever name their son Bow?

"But you aren't actually thinking of doing it, are you?" I asked, handing it back to her.

She bit her bottom lip and then downed the rest of her vodka and coke, coughing a little afterwards before taking another long sip of the new glass the waitress had brought. Her eyes were teary from the sting of the alcohol which she was obviously not used to in such quantities or quick succession.

"I don't know," she said, her voice bereft. She leaned in, her head bobbing, obviously a little drunk. She weighed a whole lotta nothing, and I had no clue how much she'd drunk before I'd helped her along with the extra vodka.

"I've heard shit," she whispered, low, swaying even closer to me. "Bad shit about what goes on during the Initiation. Scary shit. I'm afraid I wouldn't be able to take it."

She shook her head, her eyes going distant as she reached for the glass and again, emptied it.

Her eyes were bright and watery when she looked back at me. "But I don't know what other choice I have. I've got nothing left. Daddy's gone. Mama up and left us when I was just a kid. My brothers are assholes who don't give a shit about me, and now that JJ dumped me and kicked me out..."

A big, beautiful tear slid down her porcelain cheek.

Well, fuck her. She was even beautiful when she cried. A more perfect candidate they could not have picked.

I was an ugly crier. There was little about me that could ever be interpreted as gentle, much less genteel.

But I could see why they'd picked her—this beautiful, delicate woman—to be a belle of the Midnight Ball.

Frankly, I was doing her a favor. The world would break a woman like her if she didn't buck up and grow a thicker skin and fucking quick.

I reached out and grabbed her hands in mine. "You listen to me, Abilene. You are a strong woman. You've got this."

When she started to shake her head, another beautiful tear cresting and falling down her cheek, I made my move.

I reached down into my purse and pulled out the two envelopes of cash I'd stashed there. It was all the money I had in the world. But you had to gamble on the big plays, and this was the biggest play of my life.

"Abby, listen to me. You're right. I have heard about the Order, and the Trials, and everything it takes to make it to the end. What if..." I trailed off, trying to make it sound believable and natural, as if it was something I came up with as I went and not something I'd calculated for *hours* in the mirror last night. "What if we helped each other?"

She looked at me sloppily, her auburn hair slipping out of her ponytail into her face. "H-how do you mean?"

Then she looked down at the thick envelopes and her eyes widened. She dropped the Invitation as she started to finger the thick wads of cash inside.

"That's three thousand dollars. I was gonna use it for my start over here. But I'll trade it for that Invitation you're holding."

Her head shot up, and I saw suspicion in her eyes. I reached out and clasped her hands. Time for the closer.

"When I saw that Invitation, I knew it was fate we met tonight. What are the chances? I got down on my knees last night and I prayed to *God* for a miracle. My mama, she's sick, you see. She needs an operation. This three thousand dollars isn't gonna do nothing for her. I was gonna try to get a job here, maybe meet a man, I don't know."

I leaned in.

"I'd do anything for my mama. *Anything*. Nothing those bastards in the Order could dish out would scare me. Even if it's just a one in twenty chance I get picked—"

Her eyes got even wider. "It's just a one in twenty chance you even get picked once you get there?"

"You didn't know?" Sheesh, I wasn't even lying about this part.

She shook her head. And then looked down at the money I'd put on the table in front of her. "And you'd give me this money all for just the *chance*?"

I squeezed her hand I was still holding. I managed to make myself tear up, something Tina had worked with me for months on before I could do it on cue. But now I was a pro.

"For Mama." I blinked back the cresting tears. "I'd do anything. Anything, do you hear me? I swear this is fate. I believe everything happens for a reason. Don't you?"

She blinked.

I could tell she was on the verge of saying yes, so I kept on. "Just think about it, Abby. You could do it. Hop on the next bus and get out of this town. Start over, anywhere you want. Become anyone you want."

She blinked again, and I saw it. Just the slightest nod. She was starting to see it, the future I was painting for her.

I had no fucking clue if she'd actually do it or just grab the three grand and go splurge on a PlayStation and a bunch of other useless shit, but at the same time, I knew desperate when I saw it. Abby was desperate. She also didn't seem like an idiot.

Her moment of indecision didn't last long. Like I said, not an idiot. Her hands closed around the cash and before I could even sniffle again, she had the envelopes under the table, stuffing them in her purse.

"I don't know how I can ever thank you," she started gushing. "It's like you said." She pushed the Invitation in my direction and then stood from the table. "Everything happens for a reason. I'm gonna do it. Thank you. Vanessa, right? Oh, Vanessa, you're my angel!"

She came around the table and gave me a hug, but, like a smart gal, she didn't stick around to let me change my mind when she thought she'd gotten the better bargain. She booked it out of the bar.

And I was left staring down at my golden ticket. My way in.

I smiled, wiped the fake tears out of my eyes, and stood up. Time to go get myself ready for tomorrow night's ball.

Beau Radcliffe had no clue what was coming for him.

2

BEAU

I've always liked to play with fire.

Red. Hot. Flames licking the air in a chaotic dance.

On the surface, you'd read me as a no-nonsense businessman. Ruthless, powerful, and not someone you'd want to mess with. But deep down, something burned inside of me in need for danger, for heat, for an inferno that lacked in my day to day.

Maybe that was why I wanted to join the Order.

Yes, my father, and his father before him, and the generations before that sealed my fate. I didn't really have a choice if I wanted to be a Radcliffe and run Radcliffe Jewelers and Imports. But my heritage wasn't the only reason I stood in the white ballroom of the Oleander at midnight.

I wanted the silver cloak.

I wanted the membership.

I wanted it and would do whatever it took to get it.

Although I'd never show it. I'd never reveal the fires that burned inside of me. I never showed anything but cool and collected at all times. A hard shell on the outside no matter that inferno on the inside.

"Are you ready, son?" my father asked as he walked up to me cloaked in silver as a proud member of the Order of the Silver Ghost.

Nodding, I sipped from my drink, careful to only sip. I wanted my mind sharp and clear for what was about to come.

"They're going to try to push your limits," he warned.

"I know," I said. "I'm ready for it."

"I can't do anything to stop them if it gets too tough, and I can't step in no matter how much I'm sure I'll want to. You understand that right?"

I patted him on the back reassuringly. "I won't need your help, Dad. I think I've proven I can handle myself, and this Initiation isn't going to be any different than the other challenges I've faced."

Satisfied with my answer, he nodded, shook my hand, and walked to join the other members. I took the opportunity to make my way across the room and join my buddies who had just arrived.

When Emmett and Walker saw me, they both lifted their glasses in a toast. "To the Initiate," Emmett announced. "Good luck, man."

Raising my glass, I said, "Thanks, but I don't think I'll need any *luck*. Just some Trials to pass like every man who did it before us. We've all faced harder things in life helping build our empires and legacy."

"Don't be so cocky," Walker said. "You've been too busy to hang out with us lately. You haven't heard the stories Sully has been dishing. These Trials sound like something out of a sick and twisted horror movie."

"I haven't been hanging out with you assholes, because I'm still recovering from the last time I went out drinking with you," I said with a slanted grin. "I damn near blacked out that night and had a hangover that lasted days."

Emmett chuckled. "Not our fault you're a lightweight."

He was right about that. I rarely drank because I didn't like to lose control. And whenever I went to have "just one drink" with the guys, it never ended as planned. And I hated things that didn't go as planned.

A silver cloak approached, and it took me several moments to truly grasp that the man who stood before me was my good buddy Montgomery Kingston. The silver seemed to ghost his appearance. It seemed foreign on him, and yet, he was just as much a member of the Order as my father and the rest of the men clad in silver.

"I hardly recognized you," I said to him.

"He's one of *them* now," Walker teased. "I guess we should consider ourselves lucky that he can still speak with *us*."

"Whatever, shut up," Montgomery shot back with a smile as he drank from his tumbler. "You'll all have your very own silver cloak soon enough."

"Unless you pull a Sully, that is," Emmett cut in. "How's Rafe doing in his Trials now?" he asked Montgomery.

I was curious about that as well. Rafe and I would be overlapping for a short time during my stay here. I had no idea if we would see each other or not, but it did give me some sort of comfort to know I wasn't completely alone in the Oleander.

"He's doing as good as one can in the manor," Montgomery said, and I could tell that was the extent of the information we were going to get. I understood this. I knew that Montgomery danced a line between being a member of the society and being our friend.

"Are you nervous?" Emmett asked as I focused my eyes on the white grandfather clock and saw we were approaching midnight. The ceremony would soon begin.

I shrugged my shoulders and shook my head side to side slowly. "Only thing I'm concerned about is my business. Even though my dad has been the CEO, I've really taken the lead on the day to day the past year. I'm worried about just how much I can do while locked in here. I don't want to walk out in 109 days and see Radcliffe Jewelers in ruins."

Walker huffed. "I don't think you have to worry about RJ&I. When you own diamond caves, you've reached a completely different level than the rest of us. I think you have the luxury of taking some time off without worrying about the bottom line. I don't see your rich ass ending in the poor house anytime soon."

"Agreed," Montgomery said. "As someone who tried to work all the time while I was going through my own Initiation, I can tell you it's hard to keep your head in the game. This place is going to take a lot out of you. And it's not just you that you have to worry about. Your belle is going to consume every waking moment while you're here."

I released a deep breath, realizing that the mention of a belle didn't sit well with me. I wasn't one for girlfriends because I just didn't have the time in my life. I also didn't want anything—especially female energy—adding chaos to my order. I understood I would have to work with a teammate, but that fact wasn't something I looked forward to. I liked to perform difficult tasks alone. I was a solo artist. Me, myself and I. It worked best that way.

The clock struck midnight, and the Elders banged their canes against the white marble floor in a ceremonial ritual I had witnessed three times now with my friends who were lucky enough to go before me. We all rid ourselves of our drinks and readied for the next phase of the night.

The chime of the clock met the same cadence with the canes, and the deafening staccato became the only sound in the room. No one spoke. No one moved. The Elders held the room captive.

"Bring in the belles," one of the Elders demanded after the twelfth punch of his cane.

And so we began...

Emmett and Walker lined up with me in the center of the room. We stood at attention and waited. We had done this dance before, so I didn't feel like I was going into this evening blind which helped things a lot. It's how I worked. I planned every move I made in life and knowing what would occur allowed me to be able to know what I was going to do one step ahead.

I wondered if Emmett and Walker were just as anxious to get their Initiation over with. I think that was the worst part of all this. Watching Montgomery, Sully, and Rafe get to start before me. I was never a patient man, and this entire process had been slow and painful. I wanted to get on with my life and building Radcliffe Jewelers and

Imports to become more successful than it had ever been before.

When the canes stopped and the hour fully reached midnight, the room went silent until the sound of heels broke the hushed and toxic air.

Twenty young women entered in a single line. I took in each one as they paraded into the room that would swallow them up whole if they allowed it. The white ballroom was anything but pure. This grand room held secrets of debauchery, evil deeds, fears come to life, and dripped with lust. On the surface it appeared opulent and full of class. But in the shadows of every crack lurked the hidden truth.

I knew I had 109 days to discover all the truths that lay masked in wealthy disguise.

As the belles flooded the room, one tiny step at a time, they stood in a line before us. They were beautiful as I knew they would be. Ballgowns of every color and fabric draped their delicate frames, and it reminded me of princesses about to meet their prince.

Although I was far from a prince.

Many wore tiaras or earrings made of priceless stones. And each one wore a Radcliffe pearl necklace. It had been my family's gift for generations. We provided the white pearls to be the centerpiece of tonight's ceremony.

I knew I didn't have a lot of time before I would be expected to choose a belle, so I studied each one as quickly as I could. The poor things were terrified—I could see it in their eyes or their quivering lips. I couldn't blame them, and frankly, I had the upper hand because I knew exactly what was coming next. These unfortunate souls had no idea.

They thought they were about to have a chance of achieving their biggest dream, when in fact they were about to engage in their worst nightmare. Or at least... for the belle I chose.

And then I saw her.

I knew right away who I would choose and the reason behind it.

Red hair. My own personal fire that I so loved to play with. Red. I had a type, and my type was her. I was a sucker for a redheaded beauty, and since she was the only belle who had such a feature... she would be mine.

"Display the belles," the Elder demanded with a beat of the cane.

Another Elder began the procession of the belles by leading their single-file line through the ballroom. He walked them in front of the cloaked Elders first as a sign of respect, then the members, and then to us. They repeated the act three times, circling the room in an odd repetition symbolic to me of the never-ending madness of these rituals. Over and over, we conducted the same one.

I had only attended three and wondered how the members felt witnessing the exact same displaying of the belles like a broken record. Over and over again.

I tried to steal a glance of my father to see if I could read his thoughts. Was he bored? He was a lot like me—or I was a lot like him. His patience was always thin, and when he wanted something completed, he wanted it yesterday. Time was precious for the Radcliffes. We didn't have a lot of it to spare, and yet, he never once missed a member event. He attended as a dutiful man would. Maybe he felt each Trial was worth his time, and I just hoped I felt the same.

When the woman with the red hair passed me, I wanted to reach out and just take her by the arm, announcing I had chosen, so we could move on with the night. I could speed this entire process up if they allowed it... which I knew they wouldn't allow, so I behaved as hard as it was.

I knew each belle came from a difficult situation. Which was a nice way of saying they were poor. They needed to be chosen almost as much as they needed to breathe. But the belle with the red hair and in a teal-colored dress appeared to not need anyone at all. She held her head high, her shoulders back, and she could have easily passed for the most sophisticated and groomed socialite in Darlington County.

I could easily see her on my arm at cocktail parties interacting with the rich and powerful and being able to hold her own. She clearly knew how to act the part.

"Beau Radcliffe," the Elder boomed, breaking me from my thoughts. "It is time for you to choose the belle."

The Elder who had been leading the procession of belles walked over to where I stood and opened his palm. I knew he held a black satin ribbon without even looking down.

Taking the ribbon, I was more than ready to get this party moving. My need to act more efficiently caused me to feel itchy and anxious. I clearly was not a man meant for ritual.

I then walked up to the line of women and began what was called "the touching of the pearls". One by one, I approached each female and briefly touched the pearl necklace they all wore. I wanted to just go straight to the redhead, but she was toward the end, and I had to go through this unnecessary step.

I didn't even bother to really look at each belle. Fast flicks of my fingertips on the pearls and on to the next belle. If anything, I should admire the craftsmanship of my family company, but I didn't even want to do that.

And then finally I reached the belle with the red hair. Jesus Christ, she smelled good. Floral mixed with spice.

Being up close to her, I felt a sense of familiarity. Had I met this woman before? I scrutinized her face as if I had seen it—known it. I was fairly good with names and faces, so it was unlikely I would forget a face like hers. She was fucking hot, and I was pretty sure I wouldn't ever forget a woman like her if I had actually met her before. But still...there was something about her rich green eyes, her pouty lips...

Her eyes made contact with mine as I caressed her pearls. It was a shame I was about to destroy a necklace that cost more than some of these women made all year, but it was the way of the Order. Breaking the necklace was an act to show just how easy it is for The Order of the Silver Ghost to give you riches only to take them away. They had the power to give you all your dreams, but they also had the same power to destroy you with ease.

With a snap of my wrist, I yanked the necklace from her creamy flesh and heard her tiny gasp as I did so. Not wanting to waste any time—since enough time already had gone by at an agonizingly slow pace—I replaced the pearls with the black ribbon.

I hoped she was ready to dance with fire.

And then I heard the words I had been waiting for all night. "Beau Radcliffe, have you chosen your belle for the Initiation?"

I took a step back from the belle who would be at my mercy for 109 days and said, "I have chosen my belle."

3

ABILENE

H e picked me. Of course he did.

He had a thing for redheads, and I'd been the only one in the room.

Plus, this wasn't the first time he'd picked me out of all the other girls in the room. No, Beau Radcliffe had a type, and I'd had the feeling he was the type of man who wouldn't stray from it if it was offered up on a pretty, glittering platter.

I'd even put crystal jewels in my updo to highlight my fiery locks.

One night not so long ago, the man had counted the freckles on my face with his tongue. I wondered if I'd be in for a repeat tonight as he led me up the stairs by the small of my back.

A small thrill raced up my spine at the touch.

Ridiculous. Tina would have scoffed at me. No personal attachments. It was her number one rule.

As much as my confidence was returning now, it was really only as the pearls had pinged to the floor that I'd really allowed myself a breath of relief.

Getting here hadn't been a small task.

I'd had to look up Abilene in the white pages to find her address and intercept the limo I knew would be returning for her the next day. *That* information had been pumped from a former belle prospect who was both bitter about not being chosen and happy to open up after a couple rounds and a hundred-dollar tip. She was on break from her exotic dancing routine and her eyes had gotten round when I produced the cash.

If this was what happened to the belles who weren't chosen, I was that much more determined to get picked.

So I got myself dolled up the way Tina always used to when she was using me as bait for wallet snatching in clubs—smokey eye make-up and red lips with a pop of gloss. Then I curled my hair and piled it on my head since it was the feature I knew I needed to accentuate for this particular audience of one.

The limo showed up, I came out from beside Abilene's house where I'd been crouching behind a bush and swanned to the back door like I'd been sweeping into limousines my whole life.

The driver didn't even say a word, he just opened the door. If he noticed I wasn't the same woman he'd presented the card to the day before, he didn't comment. Then again, he barely spared a glance my direction.

How many limo rides and how many women had he seen in his time, I wondered?

I'd gotten myself in the door. That had been part one. Then I endured the doctor's exam, worked my magic, and voila, now I was here.

Walking up the stairs with my sought-after quarry.

I always got my mark. Always.

I leaned over right as Beau and I reached the top of the huge, grand staircase, "You don't remember me, do you?"

He almost missed the top step as his head swung toward me, and I smiled coyly. There was no time for small talk, and I knew it. There were the creepy silver-cloaked Elders pressing in on all sides and behind us.

But I'd definitely piqued Beau's interest. His eyes were on me instead of straight forward as we walked down the hallway just a short way and then were led into a room with an elaborate four-poster bed and antique furniture all around. Beau had barely given me a glance after tearing the pearls from my neck, but now I had his attention.

He leaned over and reached around, yanking the back bodice of my dress open roughly while whispering in my ear, "What do you mean? How would I know you?"

The thrill from earlier skittered all the way down to my toes at his rough treatment of my garment. I mean, good Lord, who hadn't heard of a bodice-ripper, but to actually experience it... I blinked, embarrassed of the flush in my cheeks as I tried to get back on track.

I was supposed to be the one in control here, not him. Time to tip him back off-kilter again.

"We've met before. In a bar one time. You even took me home."

He arched an eyebrow as he shrugged out of his suitcoat and dropped it to the floor, starting on the buttons of his shirt next with an expert hand. One by one the little buttons popped free, exposing his chest. He wasn't wearing an undershirt. Because he was a man who liked the expensive fabric of his silk-thread dress shirt right against his skin and could afford the dry-cleaning costs? Or because he'd been eager to get down to business after the choosing?

Had he been looking forward to this part? Fucking some strange woman provided by this creepy fucking secret society as a rose for him to pluck?

I thought about shy little Abilene, the *real* Abilene, standing here in my place.

Beau Radcliffe would have eaten her alive and spit her out.

Me, though?

He was nothing I hadn't seen before. Cocky little rich boy? They were a dime a dozen in Atlanta.

I chuckled as I pushed my gown down the rest of the way and stepped free, then stripped down until I stood before him completely naked. I propped my hands on my hips as he finished undressing.

He paused once when he saw me there naked, all but daring him. Daring him to do what, he didn't know yet.

He thought he was on trial by the Elders. The man had no clue.

He was playing *my* game.

"Remember me yet?" I asked. "Tits ringing a bell?" I cupped my C cups sensuously.

He narrowed his eyes. "Tits are all the same to me. Sorry, darlin'."

I fluttered my eyelashes at him. "I can tell I've landed myself a real gentleman, huh?" And then I launched myself at him, wrapping my arms and legs around him and taking us down to the bed behind him.

I didn't kiss him. He had a thing about that, I remembered well. Yeah, a guy who didn't want to kiss me after he came home with me had raised some red flags, but he was a good fuck, and we'd both known that was all that night was.

Until a couple months later when I found out his name.

I'd fucked Beau Radcliffe. *The* Beau Radcliffe. Heir to the Radcliffe diamond fortune. And I remembered just where to find him.

Because that night we'd hooked up, he'd been drunk. Reeeeeeeeeeeeeal drunk. So drunk that, in spite of his "rules," he still almost kissed me twice before stopping himself at the last second.

What he didn't stop himself from doing? Blabbing all about how his buddy was away at his Initiation with the Order and all the fucked-up shit that was happening to him there. And how he was next. I thought it was just nonsense.

When he skipped out the next morning before I woke up with no note and no phone number, I didn't think much of it. Just another douche out the door. Good riddance.

Had it been some of the best sex of my life and would I have minded a do-over? Yeah, best sex ever and no, wouldn't have minded being done by him any damn time. But not if he was a jackass who couldn't see the value in a gorgeous, self-sufficient woman like my badass self. So I shrugged him and the night off.

Then I found out who he was.

And circumstances being what they were, I decided to use some of those self-sufficient, badass skills I'd acquired over the years to make this current little reunion possible.

As I jumped him, tackling him down to the bed and obviously startling the fuck out of him, all I could think was, *yep, worth it.*

Even though this was not at all why I was here. Sex with the gorgeous Beau Radcliffe was definitely a perk, though.

Get your head in the game, some sane part whispered in the back of my brain as I landed on top of Beau's hard body and immediately lowered my head to suckle on that bristly, masculine throat of his.

His cock immediately sprang up beneath me.

Oh, hello, gorgeous! Mama's missed you. I grinned big and didn't hesitate on reaching down and grabbing the length of him. Who was I kidding? I was a girl who took her kicks where she could get them— grab life by the balls before it could grab you had always been my motto. So I gave in to my rising lust and squeezed his cock like I'd dreamed of doing ever since I'd last had him in my bed.

All around us feet shuffled. I'd never been an exhibitionist—I'd never even had a threesome before. Tina had tried—more like Mick, her boyfriend, had tried—but that was one line I'd never cross.

But I couldn't give less of a shit about all these old fuckers getting their dicks out and wanking off over watching me grab Beau's cock and drag it over the wet lips of my pussy.

Jesus *Christ*, I hadn't been laid in a long time. Too long. Way, *way* too long by the way my puss puss leapt back to life like the electricity had just been turned back on after an outage.

I started gyrating over Beau's body as I eased him inside me, and he finally got with the program of what was happening because his hands flew to my hips.

And then, before I could seat myself all the way on top of him, I yelped out loud as Beau lifted me, cradled me in one arm and then flipped us so that his body was suddenly on top of *mine*.

I gasped underneath him as I looked up into his clear, probing blue eyes.

Beau Radcliffe, for all his outer calm and cool, was not a man who liked being taken by surprise.

"We'll talk later," was all he said, a warning tilt to his brow. Then he bowed his head over mine, his lips to my ear.

I shuddered at the feel of his hot breath caressing my ear, lips brushing back and forth across the bottom lobe at the same time as he ground his cock against the lips of my wet pussy. "Snap your fingers if you want to stop. Because you've got quite a mouth on you. And I'm not going to let one more word out of it in mixed company. Nod if you understand me."

I grinned big, my pussy spasming at his decisive tone. I didn't nod, though. "Yes, sir," I said instead, cheekily grinning at him.

Oh, that had him riled. And then he had his fingers in my mouth, thick manly fingers.

It was hot as fuck, especially since he was finally, finally sinking inside me with that amazing, glorious cock of his.

He stretched my walls as he pushed in. My mouth went wide in ecstasy at the feel of him pushing me to my limits. He was so thick. A man shouldn't be allowed to be that thick *and* that long. It should be one or the other. Oh, for fuck's sake, he was going even deeper!

I clutched the bedsheets in my fists and held on.

And I closed my mouth around his fingers and started sucking on them as I clenched around his girth invading me. God, he felt so good. I'd forgotten how good this felt. I'd known it was good but this, this was—

My first orgasm erupted like a sudden earthquake, spasming and then shaking through my body with aftershocks. Which then just started building into another climax.

It was then that Beau's eyes shot to mine in recognition. It was still a confused recognition. He really didn't remember much about that night, that was clear. But this one thing had made it through the haze. I would have laughed if I wasn't on the precipice of another super-orgasm.

Beau Radcliffe could make me come like a fucking freight train. Over and over and *over* again. It was obscene. I didn't know what the hell it was about him. It had never happened with anyone before him, certainly, and after him, well, I just didn't see a ton of point in going out to bars after he'd, well... set the bar so high.

But I'd been busy too. I was going to get around to it. For real. He did *not* break me for all other men. He did *not.*

Oh God, it was cresting again. I was riding the wave, riding it up and up and up—

Beau reached down with the hand not still in my mouth, propped up on his elbow, and grabbed my hip in that crazy sexy way some guys have—okay, not some guys—just Beau. He grabbed my hip in the crazy sexy way *Beau* had, where he sort of dragged me forward onto his cock and gripped my hips in his fingers like he just couldn't get enough of me, like he was so obsessed with my body in that moment and—

"Oh God!" I shouted as I came, squeezing around Beau so much that he started cussing too.

Seeing him losing control was the most insane thing yet. He was a god, usually so contained, finally unleashed. I dug my fingernails into his back and lifted my legs around his hips. More, I needed more of him. I needed him closer. Deeper inside me, as deep as he could fucking get.

His body was eager to help me out, hands dragging me toward him by my hip while he lunged forward to bottom out inside me. His brow was knitted with something that looked like pleasure and pain and ecstasy as for a moment, just the briefest moment, he completely lost himself as he spilled inside me—

All around us, canes pounded the floor, and it was like our climax reverberated through the entire room.

4

BEAU

I've never lived with a woman before. Aside from an occasional weekend getaway, I've never even spent more than one night in a row with anyone else. Getting used to sharing the same airspace with another human being was probably going to be more challenging than anything the Elders could throw my way.

I was never one to play nice with others, and making new friends was not a skill of mine. But alas, waiting on Abilene as I stared at the closed bathroom door so we could head to the dining room for breakfast, was already testing my patience. I had nearly gotten my steps in for the day simply by pacing back and forth, wearing down the expensive Oriental rug beneath me.

Knocking on the door, I said, "Abilene? Are you okay in there?"

"Yeah, I'll be out in a second," she called back.

"I told Mrs. H we'd be down there by now. We're five minutes late already."

I hated being late. One of my biggest peeves in life were late people. Being late meant you thought your time was more valuable than another's. Whenever I conducted interviews for a new position in Radcliffe, if they didn't arrive ten minutes early, I didn't even bother wasting my time with an interview. Being late meant termination. Everyone knew what I expected, and tardiness was a deal breaker.

I heard the sink run, the toilet flush, and then finally Abilene emerged.

"Sheesh, why the rush?" she asked, fluffing her hair as she came out. The blow-dryer had been on long enough; I'd have thought there couldn't possibly be anything left to primp.

Really though, she was so much more fresh-faced and approachable seeming than last night. Then again, the evening seemed like a blur of insanity, and I was already trying to push it out of my mind. She also was dressed much more casually. Instead of a ballgown and a tiara, she wore a pink t-shirt and a pair of blue jeans. Simple but still stunning. Her long red hair flowed down her back, and I did everything I could to not stare at her freckles that I knew had the power to do me in.

"You all right?"

She nodded and slipped on her shoes. "Fine. Just... nervous."

Her answer made sense. Who wouldn't be nervous? I'd question her intelligence if she wasn't. We had barely spoken since having sex in front of a bunch of men in robes, and the word "awkward" would be an understatement.

We made our way to the dining room and sat across from each other in complete silence. I was happy when Mrs. H walked into the room and broke the painful lack of noise that nearly suffocated us.

"Good morning, dears. I hope you have a big appetite. I had the cook make up a breakfast for kings."

"Thank you, Mrs. H," I said. "I'm not a big breakfast person, but out of respect to you, I'll eat anything."

"Yes, thank you," Abilene added.

Mrs. H exited and the silence returned. I suppose I could have left it that way, but at the same time, this would be a brutal 109 days if we didn't at least know how to speak with each other. But I also got the feeling that this would require me to make the first move.

"I was thinking that you and I could discuss some rules." I began the conversation as I would start any meeting with colleagues sitting around a conference table. "Maybe create a contract that we agree to so we can both be on the same page. That way neither one of us will risk upsetting the other, and we can have a business relationship that will succeed."

"Contract?" she huffed, one eyebrow tilting up. "Funny that we didn't need a *contract* the first time we met."

And back to that...

I was hoping we could just gloss over the fact that I once knew this woman, and even had my dick buried inside of her. I couldn't remember exactly from where I knew her, and I didn't want to hurt her feelings. I sure as hell didn't want to come across as the asshole I felt like.

"You don't remember me, do you?"

Great. She could read my mind.

"Let me help you out," she continued. "Moody's Bar a couple months ago. You and I hooked up. One night stand, but we definitely lived the hell out of that night."

And there it was. Yes… I remembered her now.

Or as much as I could in that near blackout night that I most certainly regretted. To have fucked a girl I could barely remember… I didn't do this type of stuff normally, and now my one-night drunken mistake was coming back to haunt me.

"I'm sorry. I had a lot to drink that night," I said quietly, ashamed that those words even had to leave my mouth. I wasn't an alcoholic or some frat boy who took hits from beer bongs. I prided myself on being more mature than my years, and yet, I'd clearly pulled a juvenile act I considered beneath me.

She shrugged. "We both did. It is what it is."

"You know each other?" Mrs. H asked as she came in carrying our tray of breakfast, clearly overhearing the tail end of our conversation.

My face heated, hating that Mrs. H heard what we were discussing, and I could do nothing more than stiffen my spine and try to act like it was no big deal. "Not really."

Mrs. H glared at Abilene with skepticism in her eyes. Abilene shifted in her seat and reached for her napkin.

"We met in a bar once. I thought I recognized her when I saw her in the ballroom last night," I added.

"You clearly have a type," Abilene said, appearing pale again as Mrs. H studied her.

"Hmm," Mrs. H said and then turned her attention back to me. "Enjoy your breakfast." She then turned on her heels without saying another word.

"I don't think she likes me," Abilene muttered as she took a bite of eggs.

"It takes Mrs. H a while to warm up to people. But once she does, she'll love you forever. She's a good person to have watching your back."

"I can watch my own back, thank you."

Grateful that Mrs. H changed the conversation about how we'd had sex before and I could barely remember it, I decided to control the morning the best I could so we wouldn't have to go down that path again.

"So, about that contract," I said as I got up and opened several drawers on the nearby hutches and side tables until I found a pen and pad of paper. I then sat back down and got ready to write as I sipped my coffee. "What rules would you like to see?"

"Rules?" she asked with a mouthful of food.

"Yes, rules. For instance, our sleeping arrangement. We both slept in the bed last night but are you cool with that to continue?"

"Do we have a choice in the matter? It's not like we can be in separate rooms or something."

I could have offered to sleep on the floor, but the idea of doing that sounded fucking awful, and I had no issue sleeping beside her if she didn't.

"Fine," I said as I started to write it down on the paper. "We agree we sleep together in the same bed." I looked up at her. "I don't cuddle."

"Me neither," she said with a smirk as she picked up her juice to drink.

"Okay, what about sex?"

"What do you mean? I'm pretty sure we're going to be expected to have sex while here. A lot of it from what I've heard."

"I mean when we are alone in the room."

She paused from eating and locked eyes with mine. "The way I see it, our room is no different than the rest of the manor. Sex is on the table. It is what it is."

"Right, it is what it is," I agreed, noticing that her nonchalance on the matter was oddly refreshing, and also sent some warning bells through me. Why would she not care if we had sex or not?

"What about you?" she asked. "Do you want to have sex when we aren't forced to?"

I shrugged, looked down at the paper and began writing. "I'll just put down that both of us don't care one way or the other if we have sex or not in our room. If it happens, then it happens." I looked back up at her. "Any hard limits of what you won't do?"

She was quiet for several moments as she studied my face. "Do you?"

I hated when people answered a question with a question but decided to go ahead and answer. "I won't kiss. Kissing is for love and emotions. It changes things and could make our situation messy. I prefer to conduct business as black and white and cleanly as possible."

She gave a slanted grin and slowly nodded. "Yes, I remember that from our first time. No kissing allowed. Got it."

I annoyed her. I could see it in the way her posture stiffened and how her jaw tightened. But I could also see that she was very skilled in keeping her cool. I liked this fact because getting past these Trials would take exactly that.

"I have no hard limits," she said. "Wait... yes, I do. You can't piss or shit on me or anything like that."

I chuckled. "Seems fair." I wrote it down on the contract but couldn't stop smiling as I did so.

"Do you do this with every woman you're with?" she asked. "You do a contract first?"

I finished writing and looked up at her as I took my first bite of breakfast. "I think we both can agree that our situation is different from a normal relationship. It's not like we chose this."

"But we did," she countered. "*You* did. You chose me. Twice." The smirk was back.

I sighed as I finished chewing and could clearly see that Abilene wasn't going to let that night in the bar be swept under the table. I had to address it head-on whether I wanted to or not.

"About that night. I would like to apologize. I'm sure me not calling you afterwards..." I cleared my throat. "I don't usually do one-night stands. I went out with my buddies that night, had entirely too much to drink, and I regrettably acted out of character. I apologize if you think I didn't value you enough to remember you. That's not the case. I don't remember much of that night."

She tilted her head and simply stared at me. "I didn't expect anything beyond a hook up. Don't worry." She smiled as she swallowed the last of her juice. "But thank you for apologizing for forgetting me. I have to say that not being remembered is a first for me."

That I believed. I looked back down at the contract after I took a bite of bacon. Between chews, I asked, "So, this contract. Is there anything you would like to add?"

"I want to go all the way to the end," she stated simply. "I intend to get what I came here for."

I nodded. "So do I."

"As you said earlier," she said. "This is business. I want the payday at the end."

"I don't blame you. It could be life changing."

"Yes, life changing."

"I'm going to add something to the contract," I said, writing. "I need to be left alone during the hours from nine to five. I'll take a break for lunch, but I'll need to work. I can't be responsible for your entertainment."

"And what exactly am I supposed to do?"

That was an honest and fair question. I sure as hell wouldn't know what to do for 109 days if I didn't have work to keep me busy. "Think about what you want, and I'll make arrangements to get it to us. A hobby? Certain books? Whatever you want and need, just ask."

"Anything?" Her eyes widened.

"Anything," I clarified.

"I've heard the Trials aren't easy," she said softly.

"That's an understatement. They're going to try to push both of us to quit early. They're going to humiliate you, treat you like no woman deserves to be treated, and they're going to push my moral compass beyond what I may be able to handle."

"I don't care," she said. "We don't quit. No matter what."

I leaned back in my chair and took in the woman before me. Such determination. Such fire. And for the first time since choosing her, I actually believed she may be the right one. She seemed to have the fight and spunk in her needed for us to beat the Elders at this twisted game.

"I hope you mean that," I said. "I want this just as badly as you. My family's empire is at stake. My heritage, my future. I need this to all go smoothly."

"What's your family empire?"

"We own Radcliffe Jewelers and Imports. If I make it until the end, I not only become a member of the Order of the Silver Ghost, but I take control over the business."

She whistled. "Man, you must be one wealthy motherfucker." She laughed as she looked around the room. "I'm in your world now. I'm blind here, so you're going to have to be my eyes."

I nodded, appreciating that she realized this fact. "I plan to. My friend, Montgomery Kingston, who just recently went through and completed his Initiation, said the only way we're going to succeed is if we trust each other and work together as a team."

"I don't trust anyone," she snapped.

"And I don't work as a team. Solo is my usual choice."

She huffed and pushed back in her chair and crossed her arms against her chest. "I guess we are going to have to change."

"Or figure out how to modify." I nodded as I picked up the contract and walked it over to her. "Ready to sign?"

She took the pen from my hand, scanned the contract and signed her name, although it took her a minute to do so as if figuring out her signature was a hard thing to do. I was pretty sure she wasn't used to signing contracts.

"Done," she said, handing me the pen. "Partner."

There was no time written on the invitation we'd received a little after noon several days later, but as soon as the sun set, Beau shut the lid on his laptop. After barely saying a word throughout the day, he finally looked my way and declared, "It's time. Get ready. Strip down."

Real warm guy, this one.

It was like some switch had flipped in him. He was nothing like the dominant, flirtatious man who'd demanded my attention in the bar that night so long ago now. I still remembered how he'd approached me on the dance floor, put his hands on my body and danced in a way that promised he knew exactly what to do with me before he whispered in my ear that he'd like to take me home.

I mean, I guess it wasn't exactly true that he was nothing like the guy I'd met that night. He was still as dominant as fuck.

He just wasn't interested in me anymore.

Did it hurt my pride? A little, sure. But I wasn't here because of hurt pride. No, I was here for a much more important reason.

And it was time to get my head in the game.

I needed to get the full measure of the man that Beau Radcliffe was. And then decide how best to work him to get exactly what I wanted.

I would be in control of this situation start to finish.

Life had fucked me from the day daddy dearest split and then my mother decided the bastard meant more to her than her own fucking life—or me, a defenseless little six-year-old kid.

I was just a little too gangly and anxiety-ridden, which erupted in behavior problems, to be adoption material after she offed herself.

So I bounced from group home to foster home back to group home—from one shit situation to another.

But my sad-sack story days were over.

I was here now. Everything was about to change. Because I was going to fucking change it. I narrowed my eyes at Beau as I pulled my leggings and underwear off, kicking them to the side. Since there was nothing else to do all day, I'd spent an extensive amount of time in the shower shaving and lotioning myself until my skin glowed. I looked fabulous naked.

Beau didn't even glance in my direction. Bastard.

I frowned but then shrugged and turned around and bent over leisurely to pick my leggings off the floor, ass out and extended. I didn't glance back to see if that caught his attention. I had three months here. I could play the long game.

Plus, flirting with him now was really just a means of distraction as much as anything else. Yes, I was always on alert, trying to pick up any and every detail I could about him, but I was also nervous about tonight. If a little flirting could take my mind off what was coming, well, all the better.

Because that glass dildo the old lady had brought in the invitation box for tonight?

It was not small.

And as chill as I'd been to the real Abilene about how I could breeze through these Trials, when I'd gotten the tea from as many people who would spill, I was repeatedly warned with shudders and averted eyes that what went on at the Oleander was not for the faint of heart.

I hadn't survived this long in the world by being an idiot. And these rich dicks didn't pick girls from the wrong sides of the tracks for no reason. No, the rich picked the poor to play with because they knew we didn't have the resources to fight back against being exploited. They could fuck us, fuck with us, torment and play their demented games with us, leave us broken and then move on to greener pastures with no repercussions.

It was the way of the world.

Well guess what?

Sometimes the fucked would fuck you back.

When I was a kid, I'd been powerless. Not anymore.

I grabbed the glass dildo by the balls—literally, the thing had giant glass balls attached—and turned around. Beau had been checking out my ass after all, but I bit back my satisfaction as I held on to the dildo.

"I'm ready to get fucked," I said cheekily, lifting the dildo up as if in a toast. "How about you?"

Well, these perverts really knew how to throw a shindig. I had to give them that.

When we got to the bottom of the stairs and arrived in the white ballroom, it was transformed. Mirrors had been set up everywhere—they were mounted on the walls, hung from the ceiling, on stands interspersed throughout the room.

As we came in, a procession of naked women walked in like temple girls for an ancient sex cult. I recognized a few of them. They'd been at the Initiation with me. I guess if you didn't make the cut, you were still invited back to be a sex toy? They walked in, heads down, subservient like sex slaves.

Like me, they all held giant glass dildos in hand.

All around, the men in robes perked up. Some of them reached underneath their robes and started stroking their dicks. Some pulled them out, unabashedly fluffing themselves.

One of the men in silver robes banged his cane on the floor and stepped forward front and center. "We are here to perform the ancient ritual of tempting the Devil to this room so we might capture and trap him by his own vanity in these mirrors. To do so we must give him the most tempting meal. We must provide the darkest, most sinful debauchery. Give in to every lustful impulse. Hold nothing back."

Then he turned to the women. "Give your bodies as sacrifice to your masters. Do all that they tell you or leave this room at once. Do you understand?"

The women all nodded obediently.

Then the Elder turned and looked at me, eyes skewering. "Do you understand? Will you give your body completely to the one who will master you?"

My eyes leapt to Beau. He hadn't seemed to be paying that much attention before now, but at the Elder's question, he snapped to attention. He reached out and firmly took my chin, drawing my head down in a nod.

Then he answered for me. "My belle will obey me completely."

I was both offended and turned on. Dammit. I wanted to bite the hand he still had on my jaw, especially when he dragged it down my throat and rubbed his thick thumb across my lips.

He released my throat as the women around me dispersed throughout the room, Elders flowing around the room as legs spread and women began to pleasure themselves with the dildos.

I leaned up on my tiptoes toward Beau's ear. "Guess I better get to tempting the Devil, then."

His face didn't let anything on as to what he was thinking as I dropped down to a bench that was closest to me, lounging back, my eyes still on him as I let my legs drop open.

I'd shaved down there, too, so I knew I was silky and bare. I had a pretty pussy. I was a woman who well knew every asset at her disposal, and I wasn't unaware of my beauty. I'd always had a love-hate relationship with my body. While it was awkward and gangly as an adolescent, I'd finally grown into it in late puberty.

Some women in my business whored themselves out to live the lifestyles of the rich and famous.

That had never been my gig. Tina thought I should try it. She said we could go live in Ibiza if I could just hook the right guy. At five-foot-four, she was always envious of my long legs. I was five-nine and had only grown into some curves finally at nineteen. I'd always worn my hair short growing up, and it was nice not to be mistaken as a boy all the time.

Of course, that was what started creating problems between me and Tina. I wasn't just her ugly, boyish sidekick anymore. She was used to being the star, and when I started getting more attention from our marks... along with her own boyfriend... well, I should have known that my days with her were numbered. No matter that she was the only person I'd ever considered family.

The word family never had any meaning to Tina. She told me so often enough. I just thought she meant as far as everyone else. Not us. Not me. I thought we were sisters for life.

I was so wrong. About so many things.

And so I learned the most important lesson of all from Tina, one you'd have thought I'd have learned a lot, lot earlier.

You could never trust anyone in this life. No one ever really had your back. It was every woman for themselves.

Use or get used.

And for fuck's sake, I was tired of being on the wrong end of that equation.

So I spread my legs, dropped my head back until I could see my beautiful, supple young body in the mirror overhead, and moaned as I inserted the cold, glass dildo into my sweet little pussy.

No, I wouldn't whore myself out, but I would do everything short of to get all that I deserved. I'd get good sex. I'd have the life I wanted. The life I deserved after all the shit I'd taken. Considering what there was to be won, there was no risk I wouldn't take for my dreams to come true. I'd rely on no one but myself. For my pleasure. For my future.

I clenched around the dildo and arched my chest out. I performed, and in the performing, aroused myself.

I would tempt Beau Radcliffe. I would tempt the Devil himself. I would risk everything and bare my body and my soul because that was what you did when you refused, fucking refused, to give up.

I clenched my walls around the dildo, feeling it with my inner contours. The glass was beginning to warm up, and I pushed it in further. I listened to my body, reaching down with my other hand.

I touched myself just there, the way I knew aroused me best. My hand was expert as I touched myself the same way I touched myself in the dark when no one was looking.

Except this time people were looking. Was he?

Was he watching? Was Beau seeing the way I gave myself the best pleasure? Was the Devil watching? Did he see and partake when we gave over into this good and lush pleasure?

I doubted there was a Devil or a God, but I would touch myself and think of the divine entities jealously watching all the same. They fucking owed me. They owed me this orgasm and a million more.

I thought of the cold nights in the basement where family number two used to put me in so-called timeout, sometimes overnight or for whole days at a time when they forgot about me or didn't want to deal with me.

Yep, I deserved all the orgasms and pleasure and joy I could fucking scrape from this life, and I'd take it, goddammit.

I thrust the dildo in long and slow, and circled my clit, allowing my eyes to flit around the room.

Right beside me an Elder grabbed a dildo a girl had been tentatively rubbing against herself. He tossed it to the floor carelessly. It was so well-crafted, it didn't shatter, just landed with a thud and a slight chip to the shaft. The Elder had ruined the carefully crafted masterpiece but obviously didn't give a shit. Ah, how carelessly they could break their priceless toys.

But I couldn't deny it was hot when he grabbed the belle by her hips and pulled her up on the settee where she'd been sitting so that she was on her hands and knees. He was a middle-aged man with a short, stumpy cock, but his stomach was toned as he pulled back his robe. She swayed her ass as if anticipating his next move. He spanked the girl's ass and the globes bounced from the impact.

He grabbed her hips and sank his cock inside her. When he pulled back out again, he'd definitely grown longer. She squeaked in surprise when he next pushed inside her.

"Squeeze on my dick," he demanded. "Yes. Like that." He spanked her ass again as he pulled out and then rammed back in.

I could hear the slick and smack each time he slammed inside her as he really got going and holy shit—it was hot.

Tina and Mick used to have sex when I was around, but I always split or slammed my door shut when they started going at it. And sure, I heard plenty of people having sex growing up because trailers weren't known for having thick walls. I'd never especially found any of that sexy. Probably because I knew all of the people involved and most of them were sleazy assholes.

This was different. I mean, maybe these rich bastards were sleazy assholes in real life too. But they weren't part of *my* real life. There was a ridiculous fantasy to this place.

And for once—I was here by choice.

So I gave in. I watched the two of them, mere feet away from me, as they all-out fucked. There was no other word for it.

He was fucking her. And she was mewling like she liked it. Maybe she was faking it, but I was a woman and a pretty good judge of character besides that. It was kind of my thing, being able to read people. I didn't think she was faking it, especially when he started spanking and fucking her more vigorously. She was bucking back against him and squirming on his cock.

I clenched around the huge dildo inside me, my stomach hollowing out. And then my head turned, almost involuntarily.

Was Beau watching people fuck, too, or was he watching me pleasure myself? Was he turned on and stroking himself?

But he wasn't where I'd last seen him. He wasn't standing nearby anymore. No, the bastard had meandered over to the bar. He was getting himself a drink and talking to his buddy, not even looking my way or at the room full of debauchery.

I clenched my teeth.

He pissed me off; I couldn't deny it. I was fucking infuriated. I was hot as hell.

I wanted his cock inside me, not this hard, cold imitation of a man. I closed my eyes and turned my head away from him, not wanting him to know I was looking for him.

But closing my eyes didn't help because immediately I was back to the night I'd arrived, feeling his body over mine. I was back to only ten minutes before when he'd had his firm, commanding hand on my throat. Both times he'd had his thumb on my lips. In my mouth.

I spasmed around the dildo. My first orgasm of what I suspected would be many.

Fuck, even the very thought of him could get me off.

But I knew that already, didn't I? Him as spank bank material had been doing this to me for the past two months since that very first night. He did not break me for other men. Repeating the sad mantra to myself that I'd repeated a thousand times since that night didn't help.

Especially since I still had a huge dildo shoved up my cooch and the breathy sounds of sex noises were growing in volume all around me.

Fuck Beau Radcliffe. This wasn't about him! This was about me. Me and my future. Me and my beautiful, beautiful future and the perfect life I was going to have. I wasn't going to wait to have it, either. I was going to start having it now. Right now, with a tower of blisteringly bright orgasms that I gave myself, all by myself.

I opened my eyes and looked up at the ceiling, at the mirror reflecting myself, spread wide and skin flushed, dildo piercing my center and my other hand caressing my clit.

I was hot. I was sexy. I would take my orgasms even if I had to fantasize about Beau Radcliffe to get them. So I gave in and imagined his body over mine. In the mirror I imagined him climbing over me.

I imagined him pulling the dildo out of my hand and tossing it to the floor like the other man had. I imagined him releasing that perfect cock of his and thrusting inside me, unable to hold back any longer. He'd be rock hard from watching me and thinking about me even though he hadn't wanted me to see, pretending to drink and not wanting me to know how obsessed he was at the thought of my hot cunt.

But he'd finally plunge home to where he'd wanted to be from the second I'd kicked off my leggings upstairs. Oh God, yes, he'd sink inside me. One hand would be at my throat, thumb at my lips, shoving his way inside.

I'd cry out around him because in one thrust, I was already climaxing as soon as he bottomed out deep inside, yes, oh God, yes—

God, what did this man do to me? It wasn't fair. But oh God, I gave in to it. I arched into him, his weight pressing me back down, possessing me, pushing my limits, grinding against my clit—

I screamed as my orgasm lit higher. I'd thought I was at the climax, but I'd been wrong. It was just another ledge on my way up the mountain, and I was only beginning to glimpse the supernova at the real peak.

My legs began to tremble at the same time occasional hard spasms rocked my body with the sharp pleasure. Oh God, so good, so ecstatic and sharp, pointed. I was shaking again, more spasms, more, oh God more—

I scrubbed harder at my clit, now, all gentleness gone. My eyes were closed as I alternatively arched and coiled in ecstasy, fucking myself with the dildo and squirming against the hand rubbing my clit when—

"Knees," a gruff voice suddenly demanded.

My eyes flew up, and I was genuinely shocked when I saw Beau standing there in front of me. Not just a fantasy anymore. It was the real man. His face was pinched, his complexion pale, but it was his eyes where I saw it—his eyes were burning with lust.

"Knees," he repeated, and this time he snapped and pointed at the floor as if I hadn't gotten his message the first time.

I did. Oh, hell yes, I did. Especially since he was roughly yanking his belt open like he couldn't get the damn thing unbuckled quickly enough.

Internally, I lit up. I'd driven Beau Radcliffe past his oh so precious control. Just like the night I'd met him, his walls were coming down. That night it had been because of liquor, but right now it was all because of me. I'd driven him to this.

His dark eyes warned me I might pay for it, too, especially when I hadn't moved quickly enough and he was already pulling out his full, pulsing cock.

I scrambled off the bench and fell to my knees in front of him. When I started to pull the dildo out, he shook his head in one sharp motion.

"Keep fucking yourself with it and writhing like you were while you suck me off. You better keep fucking orgasming like you just were while you suck me. I want to feel you going wild. But don't fucking bite."

I licked my lips as I looked up at him through my lashes. "Yes, sir."

His nostrils flared like he was about to ream me out for my impudence, but I cut him off by tonguing his cock and eliciting the manliest groan from him.

I couldn't bear to tease him much more because frankly I wanted him in my mouth as much as he seemed to need it. Usually giving head didn't do much for me, but just like with sex with Beau, this was different too.

For one, there was the way he clasped my head. He didn't do what some guys did. He didn't grab my head and hold it still so he could fuck it like I was some kind of sex doll.

No, he held it and caressed my hair back from my forehead in a way that made the act somehow incredibly... intimate. And I could feel the way that every swipe of my tongue affected him. His legs and stomach tensed in response to my mouth, and it was So. Fucking. Hot.

It wasn't a struggle for my own arousal to light back to life, especially when his hand slid into my hair.

He grabbed my hair and tugged my head back so I was looking up into his face as I gagged on his cock. Our eyes met and I spasmed, orgasming around the dildo still embedded deep inside me.

His eyes lit with satisfaction and his cock in my mouth flexed and pulsed. He responded to me, and I responded to him, the hottest feedback loop. Dear God, maybe that's why sex with him was so hot. I'd never had a partner who was so in tune with me before. He got off on my arousal, and I'd never before witnessed anything so hot.

Especially as his cock got harder and harder in my mouth, expanding impossibly large. I was salivating around him as he slid out and pushed back in past my lips, again and again, watching himself slide in my mouth, then watching my eyes, then clenching his hand in my hair like he knew, he just knew he was commanding my pleasure with his every touch.

Because he was, goddamn him. Every time he clenched and pulled my hair, the next orgasm that had been building would hit. And when they hit, I'd groan and squeal and hum around his cock. Eventually, I saw that face I'd been craving—the moment he lost control, the pain and pleasure. Both hands grabbed my hair as if for dear life as he shoved to the back of my mouth and his heat sprayed down my throat.

I sucked and swallowed and sucked and swallowed and worshiped and laved with my tongue until I'd swallowed every drop.

And as he pulled back and I fell back against the side of the bench, spent and yet still spasming, for the first time I considered as I stared up at him in dazed wonder. Oh shit. What if I was in over my head after all?

Because this man was so magnetic that when I was with him, I forgot everything, everything except the feel of him against my skin.

And the craving, craving, *craving* for more.

6

BEAU

I t was fair to say that trying to run a business from a laptop, locked in a room with a woman who I was pretty sure hated me deep down, was next to impossible. We hadn't fought. In fact, we fucked. Not only during the Trials where we had to, but a few times in the privacy of these four walls.

But what else were we going to do?

At least her hot body helped pass some of the time, and I hoped that I did the same for her. Our chemistry was off the charts, and our bodies molded together as if they were created to be as one. If it weren't for our setting, and our fucked-up circumstances, the sex could easily be classified as the best sex of my life.

I knew I would walk away from this place and find it very hard to find a partner who could match Abilene. The girl knew how to make my body burn with desire. She was the fire that I longed for, and a part of me felt it would be a shame to see it all disappear when this Initiation was over. I could easily see myself becoming a junkie in the need of my next fix. My next fix being the heat between Abilene's thighs.

I honestly think the hardest part of the Initiation was not the Trials themselves, but rather the house arrest. I don't think a human being is meant to be locked in a cage, and that was exactly what we were in. We sometimes got let out of our prison to "play", if that's what you called the Trials. And as sick as it was, I actually looked forward to the Trials in some way. At least it meant we got to breathe new air. And that was exactly what I needed... new.

I sat in my chair by the fireplace that burned regardless of how hot it was outside. The Oleander always possessed a chill in the air. No doubt the ghosts that haunted this place.

Calling out, I asked, "Abilene? You all right in there?"

The woman spent a lot of time in the bathroom. She liked steamy showers, that was for sure. What was odd was that she had a natural beauty, and her appearance didn't come across as high maintenance. And as hard as it was for me to admit, the real truth behind her lockdown in the bathroom was that it was the only place away from me. It was her sanctuary, and I couldn't exactly blame her.

Rather than answering from the other side of the door like she always did, she walked into the room running her fingers through her beautiful red locks.

"Just crawling out of my skin," she said, shooting daggers my way as I sat with my laptop on my black slacks. "I'm bored out of my freaking mind."

I nodded. "I get it. I'm losing track of how long we've been here. It seems like one day is just blending in with the other."

"At least you have work to keep you busy," she said, plopping herself in the chair across from me with her arms across her chest.

"I've tried to help. I bought you every book you asked for, bought you puzzle books, notebooks— I'm trying to help."

Her expression softened. "I know you are." She sighed loudly and asked, "Can we go for a walk? I need to get out of here. It's stuffy."

"It's nearly a hundred degrees out there with a hundred percent humidity. Stepping outside would be like stepping into the pits of Hell."

"Regardless, it's a different hell than we're in right now."

I did not agree. The last thing I wanted to do was go sweat my ass off in Georgia's summer heat.

"What if we go for a walk around the Oleander? You haven't seen the place other than a few rooms, and it's really an impressive piece of history."

Her eyes lit up and she nodded with a little too much excitement. "God, yes. Anything."

As we walked out of the room and made our way downstairs, I said, "We'll start with the lower level first and work our way up."

"Are we allowed to just roam about the mansion freely?"

"Yeah, why not? I actually used to play in the halls of this place as a child. My friends and I made this manor our playground."

"Odd place to run around in. Especially considering all the expensive antiques. I'd be afraid of knocking over a vase or tearing a rug or something."

I chuckled. "Oh, we did. Trust me on that."

"Life of a blueblood kid," she murmured.

I bit back my retort but said instead, "I won't attack your past if you don't bash mine." I took a deep breath, realizing that we had walked different paths in life, and she didn't understand mine.

She stopped walking and when I turned to see why, her eyes locked with mine. "I'm sorry. You're right. That was rude of me." She continued walking next to me. "Tell me about your childhood. I genuinely want to know."

The question seemed odd to me. I wasn't used to it or being asked something so intimate. Women of my past didn't ask... maybe because they didn't care. They knew what they were getting from me and that was good enough. I think I had the habit of finding women who were as emotionally detached as I was.

"It was just me and my dad growing up," I began. "My mother died when I was really young from cancer. I don't remember her really."

I led her into the grand kitchen first. The chef was in there making some sort of sauce and looked over his shoulder at us and nodded. He didn't engage in conversation but returned his attention to his culinary masterpiece. The kitchen was the only room in the house that didn't have any real historical elements. It had been upgraded over time with the most up-to-date appliances and steel surfaces. It was the only odd one out with the industrial feel, but still impressive, nonetheless. I wasn't a chef, but I was pretty sure it was any cook's wet dream.

"Wow," Abilene said under her breath. "Our meals are made in here? I pictured something so very different."

"Like what?"

"I don't know. Like some sort of medieval witch's den or something. Old. I expected old."

I touched her lower back and led her out of the room with my favorite room as next on the agenda.

"My father and I ate a lot of meals here," I said as we continued walking. "Just the two of us unless you counted Mrs. H. Mrs. H was like a mother in many ways for me." I smiled at warm memories of the woman helping me with my homework or giving me womanly advice on how to handle schoolgirl crushes. She was always a real ball buster when needed, but genuinely loved me.

"Was your father involved in your life?" Abilene asked.

"Yes, I suppose so. He worked a lot, but if I wasn't here at the Oleander, then I was in his office. I guess you could say we didn't spend a lot of time at our house. But I grew up feeling loved. I think that's what every kid wishes for, and I got that."

She remained quiet until we reached the library. I opened the large, carved wooden doors with the ornate handles and waited to see her response. I was pleased to see it was what mine had been. Wide eyes, open mouth, and stunned into a quiet awe.

"This is my favorite room of them all," I said. I wasn't a huge reader, but how could you not be impressed with the floor to ceiling bookshelves? There was a ladder that slid around the room in order for you to reach every book.

"I didn't peg you as a book geek," she said as she walked into the room and spun around, taking it all in.

"I'm a history buff," I admitted. "I appreciate this room for all the ancient tales on those shelves. There are first editions, collectibles, and books that have been passed on from famous historical figures. The history that floods this room is what makes it so remarkable."

Rather than just continuing on with the tour, I walked over to a large high-back chair by a massive fireplace and sat down. It had been a long time since I'd sat in this chair, and it was like revisiting an old friend. Abilene walked over to join me and sat in the chair across from me.

"What about you?" I asked. "Was your childhood a good one?"

She smirked and avoided eye contact. "Hardly. At least you had *one* parent. I can't say the same."

I took a moment and studied her demeanor. I prided myself on reading people—it's how I did so well in business and negotiations—and I could see this woman was not comfortable delving into this conversation deeper. I suppose it was only fair to ask her more since she was the one who started this conversation by asking me about my childhood, but at the same time, I decided I would cut her some slack. Not everyone liked to take a trip down memory lane, and I sure as fuck wasn't going to be the prick to force her to.

"My father and I would sit here like this on Christmas night," I said, giving her the gift of returning the conversation back to me. "He'd give the staff the night off with a large envelope of cash, and it would just be him and me. We'd go to a nice steak dinner, and then come here to have a bourbon. He'd even let me drink. He'd then give me my own envelope of money, wish me a Merry Christmas, and we'd just enjoy our time together."

My heart felt heavy with emotions, and I realized it had been years since my father and I had done our holiday tradition. "May be some of my best memories with him."

"I'm not a big holiday person, or a birthday person, or into celebrations in general," she said. "Just another day."

I made sure to pause and study her again. I wanted to make sure I wasn't making her sad or ripping old wounds by talking about my privileged upbringing, when I could clearly see she wasn't as lucky to have had the same. Abilene didn't seem upset, but rather very engaged in what I had to say. She really did seem to care and want to hear more. It was refreshing to have a captive audience... something I only got from my staff—people I paid large salaries to pay attention to me.

Standing up, I said, "I want to show you what's behind the walls."

She stood with skepticism in her eyes. "Behind the walls?"

I nodded with adventure flooding my bones, reminding me of how I felt as a young boy playing hide and seek in the hidden veins of the Oleander. I walked over to a bookcase and pulled out a copy of *Moby Dick*, and the entire panel opened as I knew it would.

"A secret door?" Abilene nearly squealed. She didn't wait for me to enter but stepped past the panel with curiosity taking over. "Oh my God, there's a hallway! Can we go walk around in there?"

I grabbed my phone and turned on the flashlight feature. I knew there was a light switch somewhere in there that would turn on the dim emergency lights, but I wouldn't be able to find it on memory alone.

"I was hoping you'd want to," I said as we entered inside.

"What is this for?"

"Doesn't every manor come with haunted secret passageways?" I answered.

"Let me guess," she said as I found the lights and we began our walk. "You and your friends played in here?"

"Could you blame us?" I said with a small laugh. I had such good memories playing with my friends in the shadows. "Mrs. H hated when we did, though. We always tracked dirt back into the main house."

I tried to move cobwebs out of the way for Abilene, but she didn't seem to mind them or the dirt around us. I appreciated that she wasn't a girly girl, and her sense of adventure could very well match my own. I could see her as the type willing to hike to the top of Machu Picchu in Peru with me without complaining once.

Abilene giggled and then said, "I never thought I'd be so happy to be in a dark, dank, dusty place before. Anything is better than that room."

"I have to agree with you there. We needed to get out."

"You surprise me," Abilene said. "You're hard to read, and just when I think I got you figured out, you throw a curveball like this. Shouldn't you be working?"

"I should be, yes. But I'm not always all business. I actually like to travel when I can. But I like to do things off the beaten path. I like to explore." I chuckled. "I guess this is as close to exploring as I can get for a bit."

She laughed loudly, and I realized I didn't hear that often, if at all. I liked the sound of it.

A lot.

"I can see that. Are you sure we're going to be able to get out of here? I can just see the Elders waiting tonight with no guests of honor to torture showing up."

"I remember my way around."

"Thank you for this, Beau. I needed it. I know this is considered your workday, so I really appreciate you taking the time out for a change of scenery."

"I needed it too," I said. "It's getting harder each day, and I feel like it's only going to get worse." I glanced at her and could tell my words hit home. "But we can do this. We have up until now."

"Focus on the endgame, right?"

Yes, the endgame. What exactly that looked like still seemed blurry.

We'd had a nice day together. A really nice day, considering the monotony of life here the past month.

I was trying to stay focused, but it was hard. I had this feeling where everything was moving too fast and yet going so slow, I could barely move. Like being in a car when it's flying down the highway at eighty miles an hour, but it feels so seamless it also feels like you're barely moving at all.

One wrong move, though, and you'll end up splattered all over the highway—the way it feels is deceiving.

That was what it felt like being here with Beau.

Like the calm before the storm.

But still, today, wandering the mansion with him as he shared his memories of growing up was so nice.

And then an invitation came.

A lot of times there was nothing in the Invitation box. Not this time. This time Mrs. H carried the box into the room with such reverence and care, almost was like she was barely breathing.

I'd immediately gone on alert and even Beau had set aside his laptop and gotten up to take the box from her.

Mrs. H had shot a look my way—that woman did not like me—and then turned around and left. I'd have to keep an eye on her, just like she was on me. She'd been cool toward me ever since I'd arrived, but ever since she learned about the so-called "coincidence" that Beau and I had known each other before coming here, she'd turned positively suspicious. Which was something I could not afford.

I had to see this through to the end. I needed all three of these months, and I needed to be able to claim what I would ask for at the end of it all.

I'd lied during my intake questionnaire. I'd named an amount of money, something I thought would be a sufficient amount that most girls would ask for.

But, of course, what I really wanted was so, so much more.

It would take a lifetime to pay out.

I watched Beau's expression as he opened the Invitation box and was surprised when a smile crossed his face.

"What is it?" I asked, approaching as my curiosity got the better of me.

"Well, either my father or the Elders have decided to celebrate my heritage." He turned the box toward me so I could see what was inside.

I gasped. I couldn't help it.

I'd never seen so many diamonds in one place.

There was a... I don't even think you could call it a necklace—it was more like a neck *piece* of netted together diamonds that draped in a gorgeous teardrop shape, with one large mega-diamond at the bottom that would hit near cleavage. Diamond-draped earrings matched, along with a diamond and ruby-encrusted tiara. Glittery heels were nestled at the bottom of the box.

The last item beside the shoes was a diamond-encrusted bowtie.

A small notecard with instructions informed us that while he was to wear a tux, I was to be adorned in *only* the diamonds and the pair of high heels, because there would be waltzing.

My eyebrows shot to my hairline. "Waltzing? Naked diamond waltzing?"

Beau laughed. "They do so love their perverted pomp and circumstance."

"Jesus Christ." I reached a finger out to touch the necklace, then pulled it back at the last moment, looking back up at Beau. "What if I lose one? There are a hundred diamonds on that thing. What if one falls out while we're dancing?"

Beau pulled the box back and looked offended. "These are Radcliffe diamonds. We set each stone with care and precision. They don't just *fall out*."

I could only blink at him. "So this is the kind of shit your company makes? Jewelry like *that*?" I pointed at the box.

"This is one of our high-end pieces, but yes."

"How much does it cost?"

Beau shrugged. "Probably best for you not to think about that while you're waltzing in it."

"That's not an answer. How much?"

He sighed. "Fine. It's a half-million-dollar necklace."

I almost choked on my own tongue. "A half-mill—" I almost snatched the box back from him again. I mean, Jesus. I had bigger goals here, but still. To just hold a half-million dollars *in my hands.*

Ha. *Eat your heart out, Tina.* I smirked.

"What?" Beau asked.

Shit. Had any of what I'd been thinking been showing on my face? Usually, I was so careful.

"Uh, nothing," I shook my head and flashed a smile. Then I laughed. "Just that, holy shit, that's a shit-ton of money, frankly."

Beau laughed at that. "Fair. Whenever we take it out of the vault, the security is pretty intense."

I narrowed my eyes at him. "Don't worry, I'm not going to grab your precious necklace and try to make a break for it."

He laughed again. "No, I don't imagine you would." Then his features sobered, and he looked at me curiously. But whatever he was wondering, he didn't ask. He just kind of shut down again, like he did sometimes whenever we were getting too close or starting to bond.

I hated that he just had a switch where he could turn it off like that. It wasn't a good sign.

I thought about what he'd said about his father and their holidays. How their tradition was to eat a meal together and for his dad to hand him a wad of cash. Beau had said he'd had a happy childhood, but I wondered how happy it could have really been with no mother or maternal warmth and a dad who thought a wad of cash made for a happy holiday.

I'd had a shit childhood and a lack of intimacy and connection that I'd been trying to make up for ever since, but at least I was aware of it. I wondered if knowing you were broken made it easier or harder. Maybe it was nicer to just go through life unaware. Maybe that was the privilege of being rich—you could just bang along through life without ever being confronted with your brokenness.

Oh, Beau, honey, did I have some surprises in store for you.

We both got dressed—or, well, I got *undressed*. I went to the bathroom, my favorite space for myself where I could hear myself think and did my hair and make-up. We didn't have much time since the invitation had come late in the day. There wasn't any rhyme or reason to when they came. I guess it was part of the Initiation. They liked to keep us on our toes, keep us guessing.

I was used to a chaotic life, so it wasn't a mind game that bothered me much. The grifting lifestyle wasn't exactly known for its stability.

Last year, I was running a scam on this jackhole club promoter in Atlanta by claiming connection to marketing gurus and influencers. I got him to fork over ten grand before ghosting him. Anyway, I was up at all hours while also holding down a full-time job as a telemarketer. I usually tried to keep a legit job in addition to my extracurriculars.

I looked good on paper and have a solid resume without any gaps. I just also happened to be able to pay cash for a nice car on Craigslist and keep myself flush with nice clothes and, ya know, groceries, while the regular tax-payer job paid most of the rent.

Unlike Tina with her Ibiza dreams, I only ever wanted to get by. Everyone else got advantages I didn't, so I do what I gotta do to level the playing field. Seems fair to me.

And... well, once you learn to play people, it's hard to stop. Like the guy at the club. He was sleazy AF. He started hitting on me, staring at my tits the whole time and was obviously such an easy fucking mark...

"Here, let me put the necklace on you," Beau said when he saw me standing still after I'd come out of the bathroom.

I looked up at him, jolted out of my memories. He was tall and suave and handsome as hell in his pressed tux, the glittering gem-laden tie at his neck. Then again, the man would look sinful in nothing but a loincloth. All dolled up like this he looked like a god of the universe. Dominant, at ease, in his element.

My heartbeat sped up as he approached. *It's the diamonds he's holding*, I told myself. In addition to the necklace, there had to be another hundred thousand between the giant diamonds in those earrings and bracelet.

It had nothing to do with Beau Radcliffe himself. Nothing at all.

Yeah, whispered another voice in my head sarcastically. *Keep telling yourself that.*

I pursed my lips and clenched my teeth as Beau walked around me and pushed the top of my robe down so he had access to my neck. My hair was in an updo—the same it had been the first night I'd arrived. I knew the jewels would look fabulous on my long neck. I'd embedded the tiara in the curls stacked on top of my head, and I looked like the half-million bucks that would be draped around my body.

But still, even though I knew I looked the part, when Beau's fingers whispered across my skin as he settled the heavy necklace against me—I felt like an imposter.

Because some stupid part of me felt the Cinderella-ness of the moment. God, what would it be like for something like this to be real? To have a man like Beau Radcliffe *want* to put his jewels, the legacy of his family name, around your neck? To claim you and name you as his.

It was a barbaric notion, so I didn't know why it made my stomach swoop and the place between my legs get slick. A therapist would have a field day with me, I was sure.

But then, a therapist would shit themselves if they spent even one night in this den of sin and temptation.

Tonight, I would dance the waltz while naked draped in nothing but jewels. A girl no one wanted, now the belle of some naked demented ball, on the arm of the handsomest man in the room. Oh how the world turned.

I bit my lip as Beau finished clasping the necklace, then moved on to the bracelet. "Um, about tonight."

"Hmm?" Beau asked, absorbed in working the little clasp at my wrist.

"I don't know how to waltz."

He finally looked up at me, the first time he'd met my eyes since I'd come out of the bathroom. "Oh."

"Yeah. Oh."

Beau shrugged. "It's not that hard."

I narrowed my eyes at him. "Oh yeah? How did you learn?"

"Well, I had lessons."

I scoffed. "Yeah, of course it seems easy to you. Reminder—not all the plebes grew up going to cotillions or whatever the hell it is rich people do so they know which fork to use and how to dance at fancy parties. The most I got is that I watched *Pretty Woman* a bunch and dreamed of fucking rich dudes for money." I dramatically put my hand to my chest. "Look, wishes *can* come true!"

Beau rolled his eyes at my dramatics. "Are you done?"

I pursed my lips. "Not sure. I don't know if you've ever been an officer, but the way you went down on me the other night *sure* is my definition of a gentleman. So you're ticking off all my Richard Gere fantasies so far." I winked at him.

I wasn't sure but I thought he might have stifled a chuckle at that. Out loud all I got was, "Get your heels. We don't want to be late. And don't worry about the dance. I'll lead. All you need to do is hold on and not fight it."

I arched an eyebrow but bit back the comment on the tip of my tongue. Cause all I could think was, yep, Beau Radcliffe was dominant as hell. And annoying as it was, it was even more annoying that it totally worked for me.

I sat on the bed while I fit the sparkly heels on my feet, perfectly my size and shockingly comfortable to boot. I stood up and took a few steps across the room. Okay, well, maybe they weren't *that* comfortable, but they'd do. I wasn't falling on my face, so I'd take that as a win.

Beau stood by the door, a small smirk of amusement on his face as he watched me strut across the room as I tried out the heels.

I narrowed my eyes at him. "You got something to say?"

He just shrugged, but there was still a twinkle in his eye. "Nothing at all." Then he held out his arm for me.

God he was *fine*. Not fair, universe. *Not fair*.

I took a deep breath and then breezed right past him, pushing open the door and waving my hips as I sashayed past.

His low chuckle gratified me more than it should have.

He caught up with me, and we proceeded down the hallway to the main grand stairwell. I could hear the music from the hallway, louder and louder as we continued down the stairs.

I'd thought it was just a record, but nope, as we arrived in the ballroom, I saw it was a full string quartet set up on a small dais in the corner of the room near the marble fireplace.

The gas chandelier was ablaze, casting light and shadows on the dancers below. My breath caught. Because the scene really was lovely.

I was used to scenes of debauchery. Inevitably we came down to scenes of lots of nakedness and at least one girl getting fucked, often up the ass while another choked on another member's cock.

But tonight, everyone was really playing the game. I was sure it would end with all the members' dicks getting wet one way or another, but right now, it really was as if it was some old-timey ball—with the exception that instead of elaborate ballgowns, the women were naked like me except for elaborate jewels they were wearing.

The other women wore baubles compared to me, though. Oh, they were impressive, with emeralds and sapphires and the like, but I was the only one absolutely *dripping* in diamonds.

"This way," an Elder directed us as soon as we entered. I frowned, looking to Beau, but he didn't miss a beat, taking my arm and following the Elder.

"Pick from the selection. All Radcliffe diamonds. Your father really has curated a marvelous collection."

The man had led us to an antique cabinet and when he stepped back, I could see what was inside.

Pairs of elaborate nipple clamps sat on satin displays all throughout the cabinet, each clamp with a dangling assortment of gems.

Beau didn't hesitate or waste any time choosing. His hands immediately went to what looked like the heaviest, most elaborate pair.

Diamonds again, but with a blood-red ruby in the center of the hanging tear-drop design. Well, at least I'd match.

But there wasn't much time to really think before Beau had reached into the cabinet and pulled out the clamps.

He didn't waste any time reaching out to tweak my nipples. The room was cool, and I was already perky, but to be honest, the second Beau's fingers made contact and he twisted my nipple between his forefinger and his thumb, they hardened and elongated.

He clipped the first clamp on, and I sucked in a breath. That little sucker *pinched*. But Beau was already torturing my other nipple and I was helpless against his ministrations. Goddamn Beau Radcliffe. Goddamn him—*ohh*!

There went the second clamp. My breath was a long hiss this time. It didn't help that Beau flicked the dangling gemstones so that I really felt the weight of the clamp tugging on my nipple.

I glared at him and, for once, he wasn't impassive. The smirk was back on his lips, and I wanted to bite and kiss it off. I wanted him to fuck me so I could scratch my nails down his back while he did it.

His smirk grew larger, as if he could sense my thoughts. Because right then, he snatched my right hand in his, lifted my left hand to his shoulder, then grabbed my waist. And before I knew it, he was pulling us into the whirling dervish of the dancing couples.

Oh shit, wait, I wasn't ready! I didn't say it out loud because I knew there were eyes on us but still.

My feet stumbled through the steps, and I clung to his shoulder for dear life as he dragged me across the floor.

"Stop fighting me," he said. "Let me lead."

I glared at him. "You lied. This isn't easy. You're just dragging me around!"

He rolled his eyes. "Just count. *One* two three, *one* two three, *one* two three. Hold on to me and give in. Trust me and I'll lead. Stop thinking so damn much, for once in your life."

He made it sound so easy.

Didn't he get it?

What he was asking for was the most terrifying thing of all to a girl like me.

I never gave up control. *Ever.* Sure, maybe sometimes I liked to play submissive in the bedroom, but I was always the one really in control. Always. I just let other people pretend for a while or think they were in control.

At the end of the day, I was always the one really playing them. Really running the show.

But in this moment, Beau was asking that I *really* give it up—*really* trust him. Even if it was in such a small thing as keeping me safe on a dance floor for a single night.

It was ridiculous really that I was being so resistant. Ridiculous and dangerous because of what it could cost me if I didn't play along.

I frowned, concentrating and watching the floor as we kept on. One two three, one two three, I feverishly counted, but before I could start my next set, Beau's firm hand was on my chin, nudging my face back up. "No cheating and watching your feet. And try not to count out loud. You're beyond gorgeous and doing so well. You don't need to."

I bit my lip, embarrassed. I hadn't realized I'd been doing it out loud. Shit. Maybe I could just do it inside my head?

But even whispering the counts over and over inside my head would keep me from actually landing the steps and occasionally stumbling.

"Eyes up," Beau demanded—and he did it in *that voice*. The one he used on occasion when he was inside me. My eyes snapped up to his face.

"Give in," he said, yet again. His hand squeezed mine, gripping me more firmly, and then he did the same at my waist.

And I got it. I really got it.

In spite of the fact that it went against every single goddamned impulse inside me, finally, I forced my limbs to relax, and I did what Beau said.

I gave myself over to him. I went sort of... just limp enough to let him lead.

And the craziest thing happened. When I loosened my muscles enough to feel the strength of his intention and momentum... it was... it was wow.

Suddenly, instead of fighting each other and stumbling, we began to glide across the ballroom floor.

One two three, *one* two three, *one* two three.

Our bodies swayed and danced with the lilting music, hitting on the downbeat and swirling on the two and three.

The only thing that had ever come close to feeling like this was sex, but in sex I never ever completely gave up control like I was forced to do in this moment—simply because I didn't know these steps. It was forcing me to fully entrust myself to Beau.

And he was a worthy partner, one deserving of trust. His body was a firm frame I could cling to. The couple of times I still stumbled, he caught me and swept me into the next step. We began to move so smoothly it was like we were liquid, and I couldn't tell where I stopped and he began. The nipple clamps swayed and swung and tugged downwards on my nipples as we went, lighting triggers of sensation that zapped up and down my body.

And Beau's eyes—they weren't scanning the room or on our feet to make sure we didn't trip—no, his eyes were locked on mine the entire time. And I didn't look back down at my feet, and I didn't count to three in my head anymore.

I just watched Beau, held on to him, and trusted him as he swept me around the room, around and around and then back again. It shouldn't have worked. I didn't know what the hell I was doing.

I also for the life of me couldn't look away from him as much as I was starting to want to—because dancing was an act of active trust. Not just a one-time choice. No, it was a choice I had to keep making every moment, continuing to give myself over to his dominance and lead.

When yet another song finished and Beau finally pulled us to the side of the ballroom, I was breathless from more than just the dancing. My heart was about pounding out of my chest.

But there was no moment to catch my breath before another Elder had approached us. "An excellent living display of your family jewels," said the Elder with a smirk to Beau. "But now it's time to add a selection of pearls."

I looked to Beau questioningly—I was already decked out at my neck, wrists, earrings, and even my tits. Where exactly were these pearls going to go?

But as the second cabinet was opened, I realized that I simply suffered from lack of imagination.

Because for once, I realized that the night would be about slowly *covering* ourselves instead of becoming more naked.

But each item we covered ourselves in—all Radcliffe specialty items, I'd bet—were nothing so innocent as simple jewelry.

What awaited us in this case, for example. They were tiny pairs of lace underwear with no crotch except for a string of pearls strung in the middle.

My eyes went wide but again Beau didn't pause or flinch. He just reached for a silky black pair with gleaming pearls and, like a gentleman in a storybook, he bent down before me. But unlike Cinderella's prince putting a glass slipper on her foot, he lifted my foot only so that he could slip the pearled panties up my legs.

His fingers caressed my legs, thumbs smoothing along my inner thighs as he worked them all the way up and settled them in place at my hips.

"Champagne?" asked a passing woman, also naked and bedecked in jewels. She carried a tray of glittering champagne flutes.

Beau took two and I gulped at the sight of the delicate flutes in his masculine hands. When he held one out to me, I decided, fuck it, there was nothing like being bold. We both knew where this night was leading.

Indeed, around us, some had coupled off and begun the night's real festivities.

So I brought the flute of champagne to my mouth, swirled it against my lips, and then let it spill down my body, past my navel, and onto the pearls at my pussy.

Beau watched the trail of champagne as it flowed down my body and then his eyes flashed back up to mine.

"Look what you've done now," he said, his voice low and dark. "You've made a mess."

My heart hiccupped at the dark promise in his tone. "What are you going to do about it?" I whispered back. "Are you going to punish me for it?"

His pupils went dark as his nostrils flared. "You shouldn't play with dangerous things you don't understand, little girl."

I just arched an eyebrow at him, went to take another sip of champagne, and again let it dribble over my full bottom lip and down my body.

Without taking his eyes off me, he wrapped an arm around my waist and moved his body into mine, forcing me to scramble backwards. Like on the dance floor, it was either adjust to his movements or stumble and fall.

He was reasserting who was boss in this little drama. And like before, I was smart enough to recognize that, in some situations, the only way not to sink was not to swim, but simply to hold on for dear life to the only life vest you had nearby—which in this case happened to be him.

So I clung to him and walked backwards until he had me against a wall. And then he took my own champagne glass and lifted it to my lips. But before it could touch, he poured it all down the front of me, making waterfalls over the nipple clamps and then dramatically splashing the last bits at the bottom against my pussy so that I was a dripping, soggy, sparkling mess.

And then he dropped to his knees in front of me and wrenched my legs open wider than was a comfortable stance.

With one hand I grasped the wall and with the other, I held on to his shoulder. Even though he was the one on his knees, he'd made sure I was off-kilter and that I knew he was still the one in control.

But when his mouth latched onto my clitoris, tonguing the silky pearls against my bud and lapping up me and the splashed champagne and back and forth and back and forth—

"Oh *God*!" I cried, not caring where we were, who heard me, not caring about anything but the fucking magic silk of his tongue against my most private place and the nirvana he'd just launched me into.

My legs shook but I managed to stay standing as he wrapped an arm around my upper thigh and drew me even further and harder against his face and his mightily seeking tongue.

I continued to spasm. The orgasm didn't stop. I was liquid, melting lava between my legs, the pleasure that lit me up had turned me into a being of light, so exquisite, all the sparkles of the gemstones in the room were lit up inside me.

I cried out again and again as his tongue moved and my stomach swooped and bottomed out and the dance lived inside me as he mastered me completely. The pearls added sensation, and his tongue, and it wouldn't stop, I never wanted it to stop, never stop, oh God never stop—

I threw my head back and thrust out my breasts, the dangling nipple clamps dancing and tugging and stimulating me even more even though it shouldn't be possible. Oh *fuck*, pleasure like this shouldn't be possible. How was this possible?

And then suddenly Beau wasn't on the floor anymore. He was on his feet and the pearls were pushed aside, just slightly so they still slid wetly against my clit as he thrust inside me, hard as iron.

I clenched and cried out around him, and I threw my arms around his neck and clung to him for dear life. My life raft in the careening ocean waves that kept crashing into me, covering me, covering me. I spasmed around his cock, the orgasms not stopping me.

I didn't know it could be like this. Why hadn't anyone told me it could be like this? If I'd had a warning maybe I could have put up some defenses but as it was—

He shoved in again, so deep, so deep that I shuddered around him in an entirely new way, a whole new set of pleasure responders set off.

I dug my nails into his shoulders, but I wasn't sure he even felt it through his suit coat. But he felt something at least, because then he was coming, fucking me into the wall with desperate thrusts and then pinning me there like a captured butterfly, both of us ragged and shaking as he exploded inside me.

Then he leaned in, his breath hot and harsh on my ear. "Now you're marked with Radcliffe everywhere possible, covered in me inside and out."

I shivered and shuddered and clung to him for the last moments that I could before he pulled away because God, it was both the perfectly right and wrong thing to say.

Because he had no clue the power of a name, and how it was everything I wanted in the world.

After all, his name was why I was here.

I would give these jewels back at the end of the night, but the Radcliffe name would be mine by the time we were through.

"Now that we're back in our room, I think that a punishment is in order," I said, closing the bedroom door behind us.

A dark hunger possessed me, and there was only one way to quench it.

"Punishment?" Her eyes were wide, but the mischievous smirk on her face told me she knew exactly what was coming... what was owed.

"My family jewels are to be handled with care and respect at all times. The Radcliffe diamonds should never be soiled with champagne," I began to lecture as I took hold of my belt buckle and slowly unfastened.

"Oh really?" she said, as she took a few steps backwards toward the bed. She ran her fingertips along the diamonds draping her body and added, "Have I been a bad girl?"

"A very bad girl."

I took hold of my belt and yanked it from the loops. The swishing sound of the leather being freed, and the metal clank of the buckle caused Abilene to glance down with even wider eyes.

"Wha... what do you have in mind?" Her bravado was wearing off, and I could see a twinkle of fear mixed with desire in her eyes.

Rather than answering with words, I took hold of her arm and spun her around to bend over the bed. There wasn't any clothing to get in my way, and her firm, creamy ass made for the perfect target. Without hesitating, I brought the leather of my belt against her ass, loving how the crack of the belt blended with her squeal of surprise.

"I'm going to spank this ass of yours to teach you how to properly handle the Radcliffe name."

To my surprise, Abilene held position. She kept her ass pushed out as her body bent over the mattress. The diamonds glimmered in the dim light of the room as they brushed up against the bed. Her red hair had now loosened from the pinned-up creation from earlier in the night, and crimson curls kissed her skin.

I brought the belt down again, and again, loving the sound of her gasps and whimpers. But what I loved the most was that she remained in place. She submitted to my dominance, and I fucking could barely stand not having my cock buried inside of her. Trying to keep my focus on the task at hand, I snapped the leather even harder, watching her white flesh redden with each lash.

"It stings," she cried out.

I replied with another.

"Beau..."

And another.

My dominance craved more of the belting, and her submission seemed to call for it. Over and over, I brought down the belt until every inch of her skin appeared as if fire had licked her flesh. Her mewls and moans were morphing to whimpers and even cries, and yet her body never broke stance.

It was fucking gorgeous.

And even when I stopped and tossed the belt to the floor, my perfect submissive pet remained in position awaiting her next command.

God, I needed her.

I wanted to hold her, caress her, protect her forever and ever.

Taking her into my arms, I held her in the aftermath. She snuggled into my arms, and I knew I had to give her the aftercare we both needed.

I kissed her forehead, her cheek, the tip of her nose and then her lips. I pressed my body into hers, moving my tongue past her lips to touch, to combine.

We were kissing, my lips pressing into her soft, giving ones, and I about lost my damn mind.

What the fuck was I doing?

I knew better than this. Breaking my own rules. I was getting too close. Too fucking close.

And yet...

Something about this woman made my body sizzle. Her soft, genuine show of vulnerability and submissiveness was like a shot of adrenaline to my libido. She wasn't prissy or full of herself like so many of those in my past, but sweet and sincere... at least deep down. I saw it in her regardless of how hard she tried to hide it. Sure, she could be sassy as hell, but the truth of the matter was Abilene was a powerful woman with a spirit I hadn't experienced before, and I had never been turned on more.

I tried to press Abilene back up against the wall. I wanted to take her right there and then. Her perfectly firm and curvy body wouldn't budge an inch.

She shook her head. "We broke a rule. One of *your* rules. Remember the contract?" Her smile and the sparkle of mischief in her eyes told me she was loving every minute of this rule breaking, but she loved having the upper hand to point out my loss of control.

"Really?" I smiled seductively, looking down on her. "Maybe I need to punish you again for breaking the rules."

"Me?" she purred as she nuzzled her lips by my ear. "It takes two to kiss." She began to seductively kiss a trail along my neck. "Maybe I should do it again just to see how much trouble I can get myself into."

"Abilene..." I warned, feeling myself losing control again and wanting to feel my tongue dance with hers.

"Beau..." she countered, increasing the kissing as the air sizzled between us.

"Apparently, I didn't light your ass on fire enough."

"Oh, you did... Maybe I just liked it. A lot."

Not being able to control myself another minute, I took hold of her and pushed her hard up against the wall. Taking her hands, I pressed them above her head and held them firm with one hand, while my other began to rip off the jewels. I yanked, I tugged, and I had her completely rid of any sign of Radcliffe jewels before I could even take my next breath. My lips pressed against hers with such force, such fierce passion.

I moved my lips to her neck and began to kiss, suck and bite. With her arms still pinned above her head by my hand, Abilene had no choice but to allow me to do as I wished. With the sting of my teeth on her neck I began to shed all of my clothes in the same rush and fury that had landed her up against the wall.

I had already fucked this woman tonight but couldn't get enough. Kissing one breast and then the other, I sucked each nipple, slightly nipping with my teeth. She gasped, she moaned, encouraging my descent down her abdomen with kisses. When I reached my final destination, kissing every ounce of flesh, I licked her entire mound until she erotically mewled with desire. I'd been dying to taste her more, in the privacy of our room, as my tongue delved into her wet little hole.

"Beau..." she moaned, taking hold of my hair in her fists. "Fuck me. I need you to fuck me now."

Finally, I lowered her to the floor, moved my body on top of hers, and captured her gaze and never released it. She stared deep into my eyes, joining our souls, linking our energy.

I pressed deep within and stopped moving. Taking that moment did something to me. I felt a connection and closeness I had never felt before. I looked into Abilene's eyes and just watched. I watched the woman as we became one.

"You're mine," I softly admitted, confused with the flood of emotions rushing in. It was so much more than just dominance and primal need like all the times before. So much more.

"I want nothing more than to hear those words."

I moved my lips to hers and kissed her until I felt that our lips had melted together. Her breath was mine; my breath was hers. I felt her tongue lightly move along mine, her hands caressed, we embraced.

I moved my cock in and out of her in a slow, sensual pace. I caressed her hair and smiled softly while looking into her eyes.

We weren't just fucking.

We weren't just trying to both get off.

We were...

Fuck... We were.

Without saying a single word, I pulled my cock out of her teasingly as I kissed one breast then the other. I sucked one nipple and quickly moved to the next. I kissed, and I licked every part of her stomach. I couldn't get enough. I couldn't get enough of this woman. I needed more. I needed Abilene like I had never needed anyone in my life.

I positioned my body so I could thrust my cock inside of her once more, driving my sex deep within. I pulled out quickly, only to drive back in with a force of pure lust.

"Look into my eyes," I demanded.

Abilene's gaze penetrated my soul, demanding for me to stare into her eyes, never looking away. I wanted control, and yet her eyes demanded I give it to her. She had the power no matter how hard I tried to resist.

I reached for her face and slowly traced the edge of her jaw with my fingertips as she brought my orgasm closer and closer.

I pressed harder into her once again and began to kiss a trail of soft kisses along her neck. "Come for me, Abilene. I want to feel your pussy tight around my dick."

The animalistic fire burned deep within my core as her pussy obeyed. As her walls clenched around me, she whispered, "Yes, sir." Then she went wild with spasms.

Once her orgasm subsided, I flipped over onto my back, allowing Abilene to straddle me. Her lean thighs on each side of my body brought me closer to the edge. Her hair cascading around her face, her perfect and enchanting eyes, and the way she moaned with each move of her body nearly defeated any ounce of control I still had left in me.

I closed my eyes and began to rock my body in a rhythmic motion. The fire worked its way throughout my entire body. I felt the inferno build, hotter with each driving force, hotter than I could ever have imagined. The heat caused each moan to get louder, each gasp to grow more ragged. Abilene flung her head back and reached for my hands. She placed them on her breasts as she rode my cock with wild abandon. She went down as I went up. I moved my body faster, stoking the fire until I finally screamed out her name as she joined my sounds of lust with her own.

We rocked our hips together until every last bit of completion was removed from our bodies. Slowly, Abilene moved off me and cozied her tiny frame next to mine. Our breathing seemed to match in cadence as we both tried to regain some sense of normal.

Normal.

What the fuck was normal?

I felt my heart rate speed up and my stomach flipped. Instantly, my once satiated body became tense and stiff. Panic was setting in. My wall had slowly come down with this woman, leaving me vulnerable.

Weak.

I needed to remain strong if I was to make it through these Trials. This wasn't just a game. This was my life. My future. And the protective side of me also realized that this was Abilene's future as well. I wanted to help her achieve whatever it was she wanted. She deserved it. She would have it. I would make damn sure she would.

But not if I was weak.

"That was... tonight was... wow," Abilene murmured sleepily as she snuggled closer to my body.

With the insane urge to wrap her into my arms and kiss and whisper sweet words and promises attacking my soul, I stood up and walked toward the window to look out and try to clear my head.

There was silence in the room. Thick. Suffocating. Reality strangled what little euphoria still lingered from the mind-blowing fucking.

"Beau..." Abilene finally said softly, cutting the growing tension with the warm timbre of her voice.

I should throw caution to the wind and climb back in bed with her.

I should kiss her again like I wanted to.

I should caress that body of hers and remind her that it was mine even after the haze of dominance and submission wore off.

I should let go of the rules. Release the restrictions.

I should.

I fucking should.

"We need to stick to the contract," I said, refusing to look upon Abilene naked in bed. "As much as tonight was... hot. We crossed the line."

"By kissing?"

I nodded, even though we crossed the line in so many more ways than just kissing. At least I did. Maybe I was to blame.

I took a deep breath. "We have a contract for a reason."

"Seriously? Are you going to seriously hold us to that stupid contract? We were just joking around about it and now you're getting... Are you fucking serious?" Her words were sharp and without looking at her, I knew she was pissed.

Pissed was good.

Pissed was safe.

"We have a business arrangement," I continued.

"Are you fucking kidding me?" she shouted. "We just got done having sex and getting as close as we've ever been, and you start with the business arrangement talk. Fuck you, Beau. Fuck you for being such a dick."

Good. Don't like me. I didn't want people to like me in business. Black and white, cold, and to the point. Respect me, not like me. Business was business.

I spun on my heels to confront her and instantly regretted it. Her fury only made her sexier. "Don't get angry," I demanded. "I made it very clear from the start what was expected. You and I are starting to make this... messy. I'm just bringing it up so we can clean up our actions."

"Messy?" She said the word calmly which only made me see the rage in her eyes all more clearly.

"Yes, messy. I'm simply pointing it out."

She flung her legs off the side of the bed and marched toward the bathroom... again. "Well, we don't want that. No one wants messy."

The last sound in the room was the slamming of the door.

Messy. *Messy*.

I'd show him fucking messy.

I glared at Beau, passed out on the bed beside me, sleeping peacefully, because, of course, he was. Apparently, that was just the kind of man he was. He could have amazing, earth-shattering sex with me that felt, that felt so—

I swallowed hard and pressed my palms against my eyes.

Goddammit, I was the stupid one here.

A man promising things and saying sweet shit while he wanted to get inside you was the oldest trick in the book.

You're mine.

And then I stupidly went and admitted how much I'd wanted to hear him say it.

Stupid!

I threw my covers off and climbed out of bed. Beau didn't so much as stir.

And the second my feet hit the floor, my stomach swooped, and not in the good way. Oh shit, not again. My head dropped back. Seriously? I did not need this shit right now.

I hadn't eaten much at dinner and an empty stomach was not a good idea. I'd pay for it if I didn't try to eat something now. But it wasn't exactly like I could explain my dietary needs to anyone here. Ha.

I glared at Beau, who continued snoring on like all was right in his world. I guess it was. He was sailing through his Trial. Getting his nuts off on the regular with a hot chick who was all but begging to be his sex toy—God, I felt so *stupid* for tonight!

Screw the stupid archaic rules of this place that said the women couldn't leave the room without a male escort. Such misogynistic bullshit.

And maybe it was more stupidity and recklessness, but at the moment I really could not give a shit. I pulled on a robe, marched toward the door, opened it, and slipped into the darkened hall beyond.

My heart started to race immediately. It was ridiculous that walking around a dark house felt so illicit. It was like I was a teenager breaking curfew. Yeah, yeah, I knew there were consequences, but right at this particular moment, all their rules and little rituals felt absolutely ridiculous. Just a bunch of rich fucks with too much time on their hands playing dress up.

The rest of us lived in the real world. The one where you got hungry in the middle of the night and wanted to go down to the kitchen for a goddamn snack.

Still, I tried to stay in the shadows as I crept through the darkened mansion. Here and there sconce lights provided enough light to see where I was going, and I remembered where the kitchen was. Oh, I'd definitely clocked that on my walk with Beau.

I kept my ears open, but the place was silent. Eerily so, if I was honest. I did not believe in ghosts. Not the kind that haunted houses, anyway. No, I was more familiar with ghosts that haunted your memories—those kinds were very real. Tina haunted me regularly, and she was still very much alive out there somewhere in the world, I imagined. But I wasn't afraid of any angry Civil War ghoulies rising up. In my experience, the living did plenty more damage than the dead.

God, Beau turning on me tonight like he'd just flipped a switch...

I'd been there before.

Tina was like that. She swore we were sisters. Sisters from different misters. Sisters for *life*, that was what she told me.

I met her when I was fourteen, dumped off at yet *another* foster family. I knew as soon as my social worker parked in front of the rundown double-wide with kid's toys and junk bikes littering the dirt lawn that this was just one more nightmare stop.

I started crying and begged the social worker lady not to leave me there. She said the Morrisons were perfectly nice people and that they were fostering three other girls just a couple years older than me. Didn't I want friends? Wasn't I tired of sharing a big room and a toilet with all the girls at the group home? Wasn't I being bullied there? She'd pulled strings to get me this placement, and if I wasn't going to show her gratitude, she'd turn the car right back around and give it to another more deserving girl.

I got out of the car.

The Morrisons smiled and made a big show of welcoming me into their home in front of the social worker. But they weren't even that good of actors. I could see right through them. They didn't give a shit about me. They were obviously in it for the check. The social worker either was *really* clueless or too burnt out by her caseload to care. Dropping me off was a box she could check, and without too much of a look around, she was spitting gravel as she took off in her tidy little Pontiac.

Ray Morrison's first words to me were to order me to get him a beer. When I didn't move fast enough, he started cussing me out.

I quickly regretted ever getting out of that car.

Except for Tina. She'd been fostered there for six months already, and she took me under her wing. She showed me how to avoid the worst of Mr. Morrison's rage and how to stay out of Mrs. Morrison's way when she got to drinking.

I'd spend hours watching her put on make-up, listening to her talk about boys and bitches at school, and how she was gonna move to L.A. and be a famous actress one day. To me, she was more glamorous than any actress in a glossy magazine. She was a goddess. I couldn't believe she even deigned to spend time with little ol' me.

I wouldn't realize it until years later, but it was more likely that Tina just loved an audience. She liked to hear herself talk, but it was even better when there was a worshipping acolyte to soak it all up. And within the year, I also proved to be a useful accomplice for her regular shop-lifting schemes.

I played the distraction while she stuffed her favorite cosmetics down her bra. It only escalated from there. I never wanted to do it, but Tina made it seem so effortless and cool... and it worked.

We only got caught once.

Well, strike that. *I* got caught. Tina was distracting —or *supposed* to be distracting—and I was stealing the merchandise.

But the shopkeeper looked my way, then called to her nephew to catch me. The nephew had been all but standing behind me, and I hadn't realized he was there.

Tina ran away when she saw me get nabbed. I didn't blame her. If I'd been in the same position, I would have run too. At least that's what I told myself. It was bad enough that one of us had gotten caught. There'd been no need for both of us to get in trouble. No need at all... except I knew there was no way I *ever* would have left Tina behind. We were *blood* sisters. We'd done a ritual and sliced our palms and shaken on it and everything. I would have died for her.

But she ran. The shop owner was really very decent about it, all things considered. She could call my parents or 911. My choice.

So I gave her Ray's number.

He was livid when he came to pick me up and overly apologetic to the shop owner as he paid her for the cosmetics and earrings I'd tried to steal. And I got beat absolutely black and *blue* by Ray that night after we got home.

But Tina held me afterwards that night while I sobbed in pain. So that was something, right? She never apologized, but then again, she hadn't done anything wrong, not *really*.

Except for how it would be a pattern that would repeat over and over. That day was just the first chip, but every day, every month, every year, she'd keep chip, chip, chipping away at me. Taking more and more without giving back. Telling me how much she loved me and how we were the closest peas in a pod, us against the world…

In the end, she would drop me with no more drama, momentousness, or thought than she might swat at a gnat.

She thought her boyfriend was looking at me more than her, got jealous, and moved with him out of town. Just ghosted me after five years together. As if I'd never been *anything* to her—

Because I hadn't. I'd always been disposable. Worth keeping around only as long as I was useful.

I blinked back a stupid tear as I made it to the kitchen.

Stupid to be thinking about any of this right now. I was sneaking around at two in the morning in a kinky sex mansion, for Christ's sake. It was no time to be dredging up a past that was far better off dead and buried.

Simply because Beau Radcliffe could flip his emotions off just like my sociopathic ex-best friend/sister… Ya know. No big thing.

I huffed out a loud breath and then rolled my eyes at myself. I paused, trying to quiet my body and my mind listened. It was just as silent as it had been earlier. Good. Not that it surprised me. I was sure that all the other living souls were tucked up in their beds, snoring away as peacefully as Beau. There were no troubled consciences here.

I shook my head as I pulled open the door. There was less light in the kitchen, and it was even darker when I made my way into the pantry.

I didn't want to dare turning on the light, so I felt along the shelves. I pulled out several boxes, pulling them out one by one. Cereal. Cereal. Coffee filters.

I felt down to the lower shelf and pulled out the next cardboard box that felt like a good shape and lifted it out into the light.

Crackers. Bingo!

I opened the box and shoved several into my mouth, then moved back toward the fridge. I really hoped they had some—

I cracked the fridge door.

Oh hell, yeah. I pulled out the ginger ale.

Dinner of champions.

I was just opening the ginger ale when the room suddenly flooded with light.

"What exactly do you think you're doing, lassie?"

I swung around so fast at the lilting Scottish voice, I almost spilled the ginger ale I'd just opened.

"Jesus, you scared the crap out of me!" I said when I saw the plump hausfrau.

She was glaring at me, arms crossed, in a frilly pink robe that I never would have pictured as her style.

"Keep your voice down," she hissed, tugging the hemline toward her knees modestly. "Do you want to wake the whole house?"

Interesting. I'd always gotten the impression the woman hated me. Frankly, I was shocked she wasn't already screaming at the top of her lungs about an *escapee*.

I should be more freaked out. There were things at stake. But after tonight, I don't know, everything I'd been working so hard for...

"I don't know what you think you're getting away with, hussy, but you aren't fooling anybody."

She gestured at my crackers and ginger ale. "How far along are you?"

First, I was laughing—hussy? That was a new one! But then my brain caught up to the rest of her sentence and—

All the blood rushed out of my face. Oh Shit. I was gonna pass out. "What are you talking about?" I scoffed and tossed my hair.

She narrowed her eyes at me. "Don't insult me, lassie. You're pregnant, aren't you? How'd you get around the doctor finding out at the initial exam? Don't bother trying to deny it. I'll have you peeing on a stick before night's end! That is, if I don't wake the whole house to tell them they've been taken in by a liar and disqualify you *right here and now*."

I stood up taller and didn't bother with the denials.

Fine. She'd found me out. "You wouldn't dare. You care about Beau too much. That's why you haven't woken up the house already. Disqualifying me would disqualify him too. And you don't want him to fail."

Her eyes flashed with dislike, maybe even hatred. She was loyal to Beau and probably to all the boys who'd grown up in this place. I'd have to tread very carefully.

I held up my hands. "Look, I'm not looking to fuck anybody over."

"Too late for that. You've put Beau in danger with your lies and manipulation. Now tell me how you got past the doctor."

I rolled my eyes. "It wasn't that hard. There were a lot of girls to intake that night. I knew you guys get access to all our medical records beforehand. I'd gone to a clinic and supposedly gotten the birth-control shot there, except I paid off that doctor not to actually give me the shot because I was already pregnant. Then I talked your doctor into not giving it to me twice because I already had it in the record. And he was already so busy, he just went along with it."

Mrs. H's face went dark. "And you knew Beau beforehand, so your being here was no coincidence at all."

Fuck it. I might as well tell her. I leveled her with my stare and stood up straight.

"It's his baby. He knocked me up the night we first had sex two months ago. That's why I'm here. To make sure this baby gets all it's owed. I refuse to let my child grow up like I did. This kid will have their father's name and all that comes with it. They won't be some disowned throwaway. They'll be a *Radcliffe*."

But Mrs. H was already shaking her head. "You're a liar. I know my Beau well enough to know he's careful. You got pregnant with some other man's child, then saw an opportunity. Because that's what you are, aren't you? An *opportunist*?" She sneered at me. "I can smell your kind a mile away."

I laughed a bitter chuckle and nodded. "Yeah. See, this kind of shit is exactly what I did *not* need when I realized I was preggers and who the father was when I googled his ass. I knew I'd face all this exact bullshit."

"There's no way you received an Invitation. You're a liar and a cheat so don't try to share some sob story with me."

I put my hands on my hips. "You're right. Beau himself told me about these crazy fucking Trials the night we were together."

"Language," she snapped.

I rolled my eyes. "So I did my research. I found out where this place was." She didn't need to know it was from a former belle. "I staked you out and followed the limo when it went out. And I met up with a girl right after she got the invitation. Abilene. Then I offered to change places with her."

"You're a *snake* in the grass," Mrs. H said, looking furious.

I just shook my head at her. "I don't know why I even bothered trying to explain it to you. You've obviously never been in a tough position before if you can't understand I needed a way in. A way to find out if this man could ever be the kind of father I wanted for my child. A way to *demand* he offer the support due his own flesh and blood." I threw my hands up in the air, feeling stupid for even continuing to argue my case but doing it anyway because maybe it just felt good to say it out loud to someone, even this hard-ass lady.

"Do you think I don't know DNA tests won't be demanded? Of course I do. And it'll prove this kid is Beau's." I touched my stomach and swallowed hard. Dear God, it still freaked me out and also amazed me, realizing that there was this tiny little *being* growing inside me.

Two months in, they were the size of a grape. I'd read that on some stupid pregnancy website and could never forget it. Why did they always give you baby sizes in fruits, I didn't know. But I couldn't forget it. Little tiny grape baby.

I looked at her. "I don't know anything about being a mom. I'm terrified. But I'm going to do it. And I'm going to be damn good at it. But I need protection. I want my child to have a father, but I don't want anyone to take my kid away from me, either. And, yes, I want the support I'm due. You think I'd have any rights in a court of law compared to the wealth and power of these people?"

I gestured around us at the opulence of the huge mansion we stood in. "You think they wouldn't crush me if they could? I've been around the system. I know how it works. I needed to snatch what power I could in this situation. I come from *nothing*." I clutched my stomach tighter, my conviction growing the more I talked. God, I couldn't believe I'd lost focus for even a moment, no matter how much sex with Beau had confused things. "But 'nothing' is *not* where my kid is gonna live. They're gonna have a good life. A fucking *bright* life."

And with that, I shoved another cracker in my mouth, because I was nauseated as hell. Mornings were terrible. Even mornings that were just still late in the night. Or mid-day. Or any time really because whoever had named it morning sickness was a fucking *liar*.

But, yes, mornings were the worst. It was why I spent several hours in the bathroom after I woke up. I usually puked my guts out for at least an hour, then I lay on the cold tile for another hour, then I tried to clean up and make myself presentable the last half hour before trying to choke something down at breakfast.

Mrs. H just stared at me with pursed lips for several long, silent moments. She uncrossed her arms. Then crossed them again.

Her jaw tensed. She opened her mouth... And then closed it again.

Finally, she shook her head and pointed a finger right in my face. "You have until tomorrow night's Trial to tell Beau everything you just told me. Because if you don't, then *I* will."

Then she grabbed a white box off the kitchen counter from where it was sitting, pristinely, to the left of the oven.

She shoved the box at me. I took it from her, stumbling a little at the unexpected movement. "Until tomorrow night."

Now that her hand was free of the box it was pointing in my face again. "And swear to God, lass, if you're lying, the wrath of God be upon you. Tomorrow night. Or else." She glowered at me with her last warning.

I held the box to my chest and nodded, more than a little bit scared by this formidable chick. "Got it."

"Now shoo. Get your arse upstairs before anyone else sees you!"

You better bet I moved my arse.

Abilene had been acting odd all day. Her green eyes seemed to dart around the room, averting any connection with mine. It almost appeared as if she felt guilty for some unknown reason, or like she wanted to tell me something. Her hands fidgeted, she paced like a caged lioness, and she remained quiet all day.

The woman had me on edge.

I expected her to be angry with me. I even expected some pouting and a silent treatment. I had been an ass after sex, and I knew it. But her behavior was anything but expected, and I hated that I couldn't read her. She'd be quite the opponent in a business negotiation. Her emotions were impossible to truly read.

"Okay, enough," I finally said as I closed my laptop and directed all my attention on her. "What's going on?"

"What do you mean?" she asked, not turning to face me as she stared out the window.

"Your anxious energy today has nearly driven me mad. It's not like you."

"Well…" She took a deep breath and turned to look at me. "I *am* nervous."

"About tonight?" I said, glancing at the box for tonight's Trial. "The white and red collars?"

She opened her mouth to speak, closed it, and then looked at the box she said Mrs. H had delivered when I was in the bathroom earlier this morning.

"What do colors mean? White? Red?"

"It means you are going to be shared with the other Elders," I stated matter-of-factly. "Red means you're shared with people of my choice. White means shared by all."

"Jesus Christ…"

"It's not going to be a great Trial… but it's what we came here for, right?"

"Yeah, right. It's what we came here for," she parroted, but I could tell by her tone that she wasn't all right with what I said. "I just need to shake off the nerves I suppose."

"You haven't been this nervous—or bothered—before any of the Trials. So why now?" I wasn't buying her story.

She shrugged and turned her attention back to the window.

"Abilene..."

Still not looking at me, she said, "You know... I've been spending these days here in the manor trying to figure you out. I've been trying to see what kind of man you truly are. Deep down."

"And what's the purpose of that?" I asked.

"To get to know you."

"You don't need to know me to complete these Trials. We just have to stay focused and stick to the plan."

"Yes, the contract," she mumbled, running her fingers along the fabric of the curtains. "How could I forget?"

"Yes, the contract," I repeated. "I know I was an asshole last night, and though I meant what I said, I didn't mean for it to come out as harsh and cold as it did. I sometimes speak my mind without realizing how it could come across to others. I'm sorry if I hurt you."

"You didn't hurt me," she snapped. "I know what I came here to do. I don't need you to remind me of that."

"Fine," I said, picking up the box of collars and handing it to her. "We need to get ready. We don't want to be late. You choose what color."

"White it is," she snapped as she snatched the collar. "What the hell, it's not like it matters to you. It's just another Trial to pass, right?"

I didn't wait for another word, but instead grabbed my tux and made my way to the bathroom. Annoyance sizzled through my veins and I couldn't exactly put my finger on why. Was it because she was mad at me? Did I care what she thought? Was it that I struggled with the rules of the contract myself, and the black and white world I liked to live by seemed to gray by the day?

One thing was for sure...

This sexy little redhead managed to work her way under my skin no matter how hard I tried to fight it.

It amazed me how Abilene could walk completely naked in nothing but a white collar and keep her head held high, her shoulders back, and a level of confidence I had never seen in a woman. She wasn't ashamed, or embarrassed. She didn't cower behind me or try to wear a robe for as long as she could. She embraced her situation with such grace and such... power.

When we walked into the ballroom, the sound of a string quartet playing was the first sound I heard. But the elegance was soon crushed when the first sight I saw was the beginning of an orgy. I didn't even look for my dad. Seeing him in this environment would just be weird. It surprised me that these men I had grown up around and looked up to were dirty fuckers.

I didn't consider myself a prude, actually quite the opposite, but I also had no desire to see other men's cocks on full display either. Frankly, I just wanted to head back to the room, throw Abilene on the bed, and fuck her with as much wild passion as we did last night.

My cock twitched at the idea of being balls deep inside of her again. And maybe I would punish her tight little ass for her salty mood today as a bonus.

"Let the fun begin," Abilene said, breaking my thoughts. The snarkiness in her voice was quite obvious.

She didn't wait for me to say anything, but instead went and joined the other women. Members of the Order of the Silver Ghost were already touching, fingering, taking, and fucking as they chose. I noticed my friend Rafe sitting in a high-back chair that flanked the wall next to others. I decided I would join him there and watch the show. What else was expected of me, I didn't know, but I thought it best to follow Rafe's moves in this regard since he had experience on me.

When I sat down, I quickly saw that Rafe had no intention of having small talk with me. His eyes were razor sharp, focused on his belle, and the anger inside of him practically had an odor that reeked of danger. I decided it was best to sit quietly, watch my own belle deal with this—invasion—and move on with the night.

There were dozens of beautiful girls in the room. Plenty of sexy images before me that could captivate my attention all night, and yet... my eyes remained locked on Abilene. No one compared, and it also appeared as if the little minx knew it. Her confidence bordered on arrogance, and I fucking loved it. Those green eyes of hers taunted me. Dared me to stand from where I sat and to claim her as mine. And as a man in a silver robe approached her and ran his hands along her perfect tits, I nearly came undone.

But I refused to let her have that power.

No... I would focus my attention elsewhere. She chose the white collar, so let her deal with the ramifications of that. And even though watching these men begin to touch her and caress her as if she were nothing but a piece of meat drove me insane deep inside... I wasn't going to show it. No. I would just sit here and sip from my drink without a care in the world. I could get through this Trial. I could ignore what was going on. I could not... care.

Black and white.

Stick to the plan.

And I was doing so well with that plan until I saw Mr. St. Claire not far from Abilene begin to stroke his cock, rapidly and rough, as he prepared to master one of these poor women. All I kept telling myself was that it better not be *my* woman. Not mine.

"Get her over here," he said to the closest woman. "I want to squeeze those little titties as I ass-fuck her."

More men gathered at his side, obvious interest on their faces. More hands went to cocks. How they found this as sexy or a turn on, I had no idea. Even watching now made me sick. Maybe it was because Abilene was still too close for comfort.

One of them grabbed a woman being fucked by another Elder and forced her to her knees in front of St. Claire's dick. She yelped a little in surprise, but the noise was quickly cut off by St. Claire shoving his cock down her throat.

"You," Mr. St. Claire snapped to another girl. "Get in here. Suck on my balls and you."

Another snap.

This one was directed at Abilene. Fuck!

She looked terrified as Mr. St. Claire snapped at her again when she didn't immediately move.

This was the father of one of my closest friends. If Walker had to see this... fuck... why was I having to see this? Sick fucks... all of them.

"Massage my prostate. Make me come like a racehorse," he barked at her.

She desperately looked at me as if for instruction, but I couldn't help. I couldn't do anything because that would be breaking our contract. It meant that I cared. I would be showing that there was more to this than just a business deal.

Just a fucking business deal!

Yeah... I was a fucking liar.

When she was slow to obey, Mr. St. Claire barked, "Now! I gave you a fucking instruction, girl. That's a white collar around your fucking neck so get your fingers up my ass before I decide to fuck yours and show you what a real man feels like!"

I needed to look away. No way could I just sit here and watch Abilene finger Walker's dad's ass. I could only take so much. But his shout toward her forced me to redirect my eyes in their direction.

"Jesus, I didn't say shove your fingers up my ass," Mr. St. Claire roared, turning so violently he yanked his cock away from the other women's servicing mouths. "I said massage my prostate."

Abilene just blinked up in shock and what looked a little like fear. She was afraid. She was so fucking afraid, and it took all my might not to storm toward her and kick St. Claire's hairy ass in front of all. But he was an Elder. This was a Trial. We had to stay on task or risk losing it all...

Then Mr. St. Claire rolled his eyes. "Jesus Christ, Beau, maybe teach your belle some of the fucking basics of pleasuring a man. Uma, get back there and show her where a man's fucking prostate is." Mr. St. Claire glared at me. "Consider this a fucking favor."

I did my best to give an uninterested smirk and raised my bourbon glass in toast. It took all I could manage not to stand up and scream out with rage.

Why was I feeling rage?

Luckily as I was reaching my max, Montgomery came up to me and said, "Deep breath."

"I'm fine," I lied as I took another sip of my drink. "All part of the Trial. Focus on the endgame."

"If it makes you better saying that out loud, then by all means. But I know you, bro. This is ripping you up inside."

"Like I said... I'm fine."

But I wasn't. I wasn't!

Don't fucking touch what is mine!

There were no rules for the night that I was aware of. Who said I had to remain seated and watch? Clearly, a white collar meant others could touch the women as they chose but beware to the man who gets in the way of my belle pleasuring *me*. Me.

Marching over to her, I took a handful of her crimson hair and pushed her down to her knees. The forceful action was enough to have St. Claire chuckling.

"Let me teach my belle a lesson," I said, hoping that being aggressive toward Abilene would distract St. Claire without offending him. "She should know how to pleasure an Elder, and now that she failed at that, there will be consequences."

Walker's dad laughed again and focused his attention on another woman. "By all means. She's all yours."

Unbuttoning my pants, freeing my cock, and looking down upon her startled face, I ordered, "Suck my dick. Now."

I didn't ask. I wasn't going to be polite. I wanted everyone in this room—including Abilene—to know she was mine. Mine.

Fisting my cock, I brought it to her lips at the same time I guided her head to me by her hair, which I had yet to release. This wasn't going to be about love. It was not about affection. This wasn't going to be a moment of connection. This was about lust. Primal, animalistic claiming of what belonged to me.

And Abilene knew it. Because without pause, she parted her lips and ran her tongue along the head of my dick, never breaking her stare with mine.

"Taste all of me," I groaned as I tugged her hair harder.

Obeying my command, Abilene took my hardened cock fully in her mouth and began bobbing her head up and down with a force and friction that nearly made my legs buckle.

Women mewled around me.

Men moaned in erotic pleasure.

But all I could focus on was the way her lips looked as they ran up and down the flesh of my cock with the purpose to please.

"Deeper," I moaned, driving my dick to the back of her throat. "Deep throat me like the dirty girl you are."

As if she were under a submissive spell, the back of her throat seemed to open up and my dick slid in even further. She didn't gag, but tears blurred the green in her eyes, and yet she only lowered her mouth more.

So fucking deep.

So fucking tight.

Not being able to take it any longer, I pulled out of her mouth. I considered releasing my cum all over her flawless chest, and even on her face so that no member of the Order would even ask the question of whom she belonged to, but I wanted more. I wanted to fully claim her in every way, and every place. And there was still one hole I had yet to make mine.

Not wanting to be in the center of the room anymore, I lifted her from her knees and guided her over to a fainting couch set up near the fireplace. Lucky for me, I noticed several bottles of lube on a nearby table and picked one up on the way.

"I'm going to fuck your ass," I announced, again not asking, but telling.

Abilene didn't say anything, but she nearly tripped on her own feet as we walked over to the couch.

Not wasting another minute, I bent her over the couch, coated my finger with lube and placed it against her tiny hole that would soon be mine. She gasped as my finger breached the opening, but she didn't break from the position I had her in over the edge of the couch with her ass out on full display.

"You should be thanking me that I'm willing to stretch you before I plunge my dick deep inside."

"Christ," she hissed as she moaned and tensed her body.

"Relax," I ordered as I moved my finger in and out of her, easing my way from side to side with each thrust.

"Just fuck my ass already," she said as her hole tightened around my finger.

With my free hand, I spanked her ass hard. "You don't give the orders here." I spanked her again, and again. "I do."

I thrust my finger a little deeper and with more force. Liking how her back arched and little whimpers escaped from her lips as I did so, I continued to finger fuck her. I swatted her over and over, reddening the flesh of her ass.

Needing to be inside her more than I needed to take my next breath, I pulled out my finger, lubed up my cock, and pushed it at her entrance pausing just enough to say, "This is going to hurt."

Taking hold of her hips, I pushed my dick past her tight entrance and spread her wide as I did so.

Her gasps and tiny mewls told me that my warning was spot on. But rather than trying to wiggle free, or crying out for me to stop, the devilish woman pushed against me, driving me even deeper inside. She liked the pain. She liked the claiming of her ass. I could feel it in the way she moved against me.

I spanked her ass one more time as a warning that, though I appreciated her movements, I was in control. I would be deciding how fast and how deep we would go.

"Beau!" I heard from behind me.

I snapped my neck to see Mrs. H charging toward me.

Still being balls deep inside Abilene's ass, Mrs. H approached us without any hesitation and whispered in my ear, "How dare you slap a girl in her condition?"

Slap?

Her condition?

Mrs. H?

Quickly yanking my cock out of Abilene and tucking it into my pants, I struggled to make sense of what was going on. Abilene turned and sat on the couch, pulling her legs up to her chest to try to hide her body from Mrs. H's stare.

"What the fu— are you doing here?" I said, looking around the room to see if anyone else noticed that the house mother of the Oleander was in the ballroom in the middle of a goddamn orgy. It appeared that everyone else was far too busy to notice. Abilene and I were the only ones blessed with this awkward moment.

"You're damn near rooting her like a pig!" Mrs. H said as she put her hands on her hips. "I'm not one to treat women as delicate china while pregnant, but I do expect you be a little more careful. Especially since we don't know how the baby is doing without the doctor checking her first. She hasn't been cleared for... activities."

I stole a glance at Abilene whose eyes were wide, and she was shaking her head at Mrs. H.

"What the hell are you talking about? Baby? Pregnant?" My voice was low enough so only

Abilene and maybe Mrs. H could hear me. "Are you fucking pregnant?"

Abilene's lip trembled and loose curls hung around her face, shielding her face some, but not enough. I could see the answer written all over it.

"Pregnant?" Just saying the word scorched my tongue. "Pregnant."

"I tried to tell you." She looked at Mrs. H. "I was going to tell him today."

Mrs. H took me by the arm and whispered in my ear. "Get her out of here before anyone notices a scene."

My ears rang, blocking out the sound of the classical music mixed with sounds of orgasms and conquests. I agreed with Mrs. H. We needed to get out of here immediately. I needed air. I needed to come to terms with what I was hearing.

Pregnant...

"What the hell did she mean? You can't be pregnant!" Beau all but shouted after dragging me back up to our bedroom and slamming the door behind us.

I think the Elders might have had something to say about our disappearing so suddenly, but right as we were leaving, there was some other disturbance. I'd just glimpsed the other Initiate standing up and calling out the Elders right as Beau pulled me from the room by my elbow.

I stared Beau down now that we were alone in the bedroom. My emotions were all over the place after everything that had just happened downstairs. "I sure *can* be pregnant. I am. And the baby's yours. From the first night we slept together two months ago."

If I thought Beau had looked pissed before, it was nothing to the way his face turned cherry red now.

He charged me.

I yelped and tried to run, but there was nowhere to go. Before I could escape, he had my back up against the door.

His hand came to my neck. He didn't squeeze, he just kept it there, pinning me in place exactly where he wanted.

"You've been lying to me from the beginning," he seethed through his teeth.

I grabbed the wrist of his hand at my throat and yanked it downwards and off, then shoved him hard in the chest.

"No, I just wanted to see what kind of father my child would have. And now I'm seeing you in all your true colors. So thank you."

"Stop saying that. If you *are* even pregnant, we both know it's not mine. I never have sex without a condom."

I raised my eyebrows at him, and he waved an impatient hand through the air. "Apart from in here. I was assured you'd be on foolproof birth-control while in the mansion."

"I am," I sneered. "I'm already pregnant."

"With some other man's bastard. That you're trying to pass off as mine. I'm not that much of a fucking idiot. You think desperate whores haven't tried to target me before?"

Desperate who—

"You self-entitled son of a bitch!"

He wasn't the only one who could get pissed. "I didn't know who you were that night at the bar! And guess what, Mr. I'm Always So Responsible, you *didn't* wear a condom that night. You didn't even bother to ask me for one, either. We were both drunk off our asses and so damn hot for each other, we barely got into my apartment before you had me shoved up against the wall with your dick in me. Remember that? Oh, right, no, you don't. Doesn't stop it from being any less true. Especially since your little seed dump in my vag resulted in a freaking *kid*. And wasn't *that* a delightful little surprise to discover six weeks later."

He'd pulled back and crossed his arms over his chest, his face an ice sculpture. "Are you done?" he asked coolly.

"Am I done?" I asked, getting more pissed the calmer he went. "No, no I'm not. Because after I found out who you were, I *tried* to call you. But guess who wouldn't put through the call of some nobody who claimed they'd once had a date with you. In fact, turns out you're fucking *impossible* to get to. Mr. Untouchable. But I was goddamned sure my kid wasn't gonna grow up like me. Or get taken away from me, either. They're going to have their father's last name and the life they deserve, and I'm going to be their mother."

Beau's control snapped, and it was a beautiful thing to observe. His finger came out and he pointed it right in my face. "Then I guess you better go to the bar and assault the bouncer or the bartender or whoever else you fucked since it seems to be so easy to get between those legs of yours."

I fucking slapped him.

Hard.

And when I reared back to slap him a second time, his own hand shot out and snatched my arm by the wrist again.

I pulled against him, but he was strong and when he wouldn't let go, I was stuck there, arm in the air, held in his iron grip.

"You're the only one I've slept with in the last year, you stupid fucking *bastard*!"

His eyes widened at that and his grip loosened. I yanked my arm back and he let me go. I stormed away from him but didn't get two steps before he was stopping me again.

His grip wasn't as firm this time, and I immediately yanked away. His features were confused, cautious, and it was not a normal look on the usually confident Beau's face.

"Say you're telling the truth..." He drifted off like he couldn't even finish the thought, it was *that* incomprehensible.

I shook my head in disgust at him. "Jesus Christ, do you think I'm stupid? I know you'll want DNA testing to prove the baby's yours. And you can have that. All the tests you want. Because I know what they'll say. Do you think I would fucking come here and do all this if I weren't sure you were the father?" I waved at the mansion around us.

I guess that was when it really hit, because Beau blinked, and took a stumbling step backwards, then blinked some more. "A baby? I'm going to be a dad?"

He ran his hand through his hair, still looking like he'd just been hit by the Mack truck of all news. Which I guess he had.

"Yeah," I huffed out a sardonic laugh. "I wasn't exactly ready for the news either. I never thought I'd—"

But then my hands went to my waist. It was still flat, but sometimes at night I would lie down and touch my tummy and just imagine the little being in there. The heartbeat thrumming away. What it would feel like to hold a baby in my arms in less than seven months. My son or daughter.

I still could barely wrap my head around it.

Jesus, I was gonna screw this kid up. I probably already was doing a bang up job of it. I looked over at Beau. He was still blinking, his mouth opening and closing like he was about to say something, but then his eyes would twitch again, and he'd stay silent. It was like watching a robot short-circuit. I could all but see the readout flashing across his forehead: Does not compute! Does not compute!

Oh God, this was going to be a disaster. It already was. I'd fucked everything up.

Which was when I felt that tell-tale sick tingle underneath my tongue, and then the nauseous feeling sweeping through my stomach.

Oh shit.

I fled for the bathroom, slamming and locking the door shut behind me, then barely made it to the toilet in time before losing the meager contents of the lunch I'd pecked at and all the water I'd drunk to stay hydrated.

Almost immediately, there was a banging at the door. "Abilene. Abby! Open up. Let me in!"

I grabbed the toilet bowl and retched again, spitting up bile.

I felt hot and sweaty all over and my eyes teared up as I reached for some toilet paper to wipe my face and mouth.

"Abilene! I'm serious, open this door right now!"

I flopped onto the cool tile floor by the toilet and sank back against the wall. I let my head drop back until I was staring sightlessly at the ceiling.

"Abilene!" *Bang bang bang bang.*

I put my weak hands to my head, then shouted at the door. "Go away! This parasite you put inside me makes me barf three times a fucking day! You can wait your goddamned turn for the toilet!"

Then I groaned and rubbed my belly. "I'm sorry, baby. I don't really think you're a parasite. You're amazing, I know it already. Your daddy is just an asshole who needs a beat-down from Mommy. But Mommy's too tired for the beat-down right now."

I let my head sink back against the wall.

But Beau wasn't letting up and was all but banging the door off the wall. When he threatened to do just that, I finally yelled, "Fine!" and struggled to drag my weak and shaky ass off the floor.

I half-hobbled, half-crawled over to the door, unlocked it and flung it open. But the movement had been too much, too soon, and then I was crawling back to the toilet, hugging the lid, and retching even more. Barely anything came out, but each time it was an entire body spasm. By the time my body was done trying to expel what was no longer in it to be expelled anyway, I was a sweaty, teary mess.

Which was when I realized there was a body behind me. And strong hands holding back my hair. Beau was rubbing my back and holding my hair while I—

If I was a teary mess before, it was nothing to the tears that exploded at this unexpected, gentle action.

Beau as a cold ice-man asshole, I could handle. Not this, not this—

"Shhhh," he said, turning me and pulling me into his arms. "Shhhh."

And then, as I lay limp and exhausted and completely spent by the evening and its spectacular culmination, suddenly I was floating.

Beau had lifted me up. He cradled me in his arms. And then before I'd quite comprehended what was happening or how absolutely *heavenly* it felt to be held so secure in his arms like that, he was laying me gently on the bed.

I blinked my eyes open, and his face was soft and distressed with concern. And then I felt his hands around my body again. Was he— Was he really... *tucking me in*?

But yes. Yes, Beau Radcliffe had just been compassionate and gentle, putting me in bed and tucking me in when I'd been sick.

"Shhh. You need to get some rest. We'll talk more when you wake up. You don't have to worry about a thing anymore. If this child is really mine, they will never want for anything. *Ever*."

So I fell asleep, feeling that no matter how much else I'd screwed up along the way, it seemed like I may have accomplished at least one thing.

My child would be a Radcliffe.

I walked over to the window to try to keep my eyes off Abilene—something I struggled to do as every hour in the Oleander ticked by at an agonizingly slow pace. I knew the only way I was going to get through these days was to stay focused on the endgame. No distractions. Chicks fucked things up for me in my life, and I sure as hell wasn't going to allow this one to mess up what was the most important test ever... at least that had been the plan.

But her news just threw me for a loop. I couldn't process her words, I couldn't picture the future. I couldn't plan my next step. Complete chaos.

The goal of the Order was to break the belle.

Not save the belle.

Not fall for the belle.

Not live happily ever after with the belle.

But now there was a baby to think of. The rules of the game just drastically changed.

We hadn't been in the manor long, and I'd already found myself struggling, which wasn't a good sign. I had come in so confident I could handle this secret society shit, that it would be just another box to check in my confident march toward the future I'd always seen for myself. But now this pregnancy...

I was pretty sure I wasn't the first person to get a belle pregnant in the lifetime of the Order, but how I handle it will be the key of pleasing the Elders or risking everything. I just wasn't sure what needed to be done or how to do it that would be considered "right" and "proper".

And now that I knew Abilene was pregnant, should I pull us out? Did I let the Elders know she was in no way fit for... further activities? No... I needed to focus on completing each and every Trial no matter what was thrown my way. Whatever was thrown *our* way. As long as it wouldn't hurt the baby.

Thinking of all this was going to drive me mad.

Luckily, I saw a distraction down below my window. Rafe walked slowly toward the cemetery, and even though I knew his reason for doing so, I decided to leave our room for a quick minute and go say hello... or goodbye since I knew his Initiation was complete.

Mrs. H had told me this morning that it would just be me and Abilene now, though she remained mum on the details. She had come in to check on Abilene, the baby, and on me. I had told her I wasn't in a position to discuss this right now, which luckily the woman understood and left us with our breakfast.

"I'll be right back," I said to Abilene, who was watching an old black and white movie on a little TV I'd managed to get for her.

I could tell she didn't want to have a deep conversation any more than I did, and she, too, was trying to avoid making eye contact with me.

She looked up surprised. "Where are you going? We aren't allowed to leave the room alone."

"No," I said as I quickly put on my shoes. "*You*, as the belle, aren't supposed to leave. I'll only be a second. I'm going to go say goodbye to my buddy." I looked up and saw the news of being left alone upset her. "Don't worry. I'll only be a couple of minutes."

Not waiting for her to argue or beg to come along, I quickly left the room, jogged down the hallway, and out of the house to catch up with Rafe who was nearly at the top of the hill.

As I approached where he stood in front of a grave, I overheard him talking and decided to give him the space to say what he came to say.

"I should have come here sooner," Rafe said as he stood before his brother, Timothy's, headstone. "It was guilt that kept me away. I always thought it was me who put you here, and although I still wish I had picked up that fucking phone..."

He took a deep breath and paused for several moments. "Well, I did it. I passed the Initiation. I wanted to make Dad proud, and I wanted to honor your name. I hope I did. Can you believe it? I'm a member of The Order of the Silver Ghost. I'll be wearing one of those cloaks and being part of it all."

Rafe looked down at his feet and kicked at a root before adding, "I miss you, brother. I do. But I also have some news. Fallon Perry... remember her?

Yeah, well, you won't believe it, but I love her." He laughed. "Yeah, you always teased me for having a crush on her back when we were kids. And you were right as much as I hate to admit that you were. Anyway... I hope to have her in my life forever, and it gives me a sort of comfort knowing you knew her and would approve. I know you would approve."

His voice hitched, and he looked up at the sky. "I fucking miss you."

"He was a good man," I said as I walked up to Rafe and put my hand on his shoulder in comfort. "I always looked up to Tim. I'm sure he would be really proud of the man you became."

Rafe nodded. "He was a good man, and I hope so. I really do hope I served his memory well." He then looked at me. "You escaped the den of vipers for a bit?"

I shrugged and put my hands in my pockets still staring at Tim's headstone. "This shit is wild. I can tell you that. Nothing Sully told me prepared me for this." I glanced at Rafe and added, "I'm happy you completed the Initiation. Congrats. I hope I can do the same."

Rafe chuckled. "You've just begun. Trust me. It gets so much worse."

"But you passed it, so that's good."

"I'm not sure how. There were times I nearly quit. Frankly, I owe a lot of it to Fallon. That girl kept me sane."

"You are so lucky to have had someone you actually know as your belle. Being locked up with a complete stranger is bizarre. It's like the worst blind date in history over and over again. I think it's harder than the actual Trials have been."

"How are you getting along with your belle?" Rafe asked.

Rafe had enough on his plate. He didn't need me to unload all my shit on him. And I wasn't prepared to discuss the pregnancy yet with anyone. I still couldn't believe it... It was like I was in shock or something. For now, the secret of the belle and the baby would have to remain locked inside of me.

"Okay... not like you and Fallon, but fine. She's a good fuck and a hot piece of ass, so I guess I should consider myself lucky. But when these 109 days are over, I'm moving forward and not looking back."

Maybe I was lying... okay... I was lying. But it felt good to say. Wouldn't it be great if it were that simple? If I could just block this nightmare from my life and continue on as planned? But the reality was that nothing was going to be the same again.

Rafe laughed and patted me on the shoulder blade. "You tell yourself whatever you want. There is no way in hell anyone can walk out of this place, enduring what we do for so long, and not form some sort of connection. No way. That belle in there is going to fuck with your mind and with your heart. No use fighting it."

"Your situation is different," I said. "But I'm happy for you. Let's hope the rest of us pass the Trials and not end up pulling a Sully."

"You got this," Rafe encouraged as he turned to leave the cemetery. "I need to get going. Fallon's waiting for me."

I walked beside him, trying not to focus on the large manor before me. It reminded me of something Stephen King would write in one of his horror novels. The moment of fresh air and the break from it all made me feel normal again. Human. Even if only for a brief moment.

"Do you want a piece of advice?" Rafe asked as we made it down the hill.

"Sure. Anything to help get past this."

"Don't be a dick." He patted my back good-heartedly and smiled. "I know you. You don't do relationships. You keep to yourself. And you can be a super dick. I say that with love, but being a dick isn't going to help you or your belle. So, don't be a dick."

I smirked, and shoved Rafe playfully. "Got it. Don't be a dick." As we got closer to the manor, I asked the question I had been wanting to ask since I left the room. "Why do we do this? I mean... why do we care? Why is the Order so important?"

"Inherited malice," Rafe said simply. "It's in our blood. No choice."

How true his words were.

And yet, the word inheritance... It made me think of the child Abilene claimed was mine, growing in her belly. A thought which I quickly shut down.

As we parted ways, I made my way back to our room. It wasn't fair for me to leave Abilene inside alone, while I got to at least see the sun and breathe some non-toxic air. I should at least offer the same opportunity to her.

When I entered the room, Abilene was pacing from one side to the other, clearly agitated. She spun to face me, and before I could even say a word, she said, "Okay, we can't just ignore the obvious. We can't just avoid confrontation today."

"Agreed," I stated as I pointed to her shoes. "Let's go for a walk. It's not hot out yet, and I think it will do us both some good."

We silently made our way out of the Oleander, and Rafe's words rang in my ears. "I'm sorry for being a dick last night. My first reaction to the news of the baby isn't something I'm proud of. I'm sorry."

She inhaled deeply as we began to walk along the oak trees that offered sporadic shade to help ease the summer temperature. "I know it was a shock. But I also swear I'm not lying. The baby's yours."

"I believe you."

And I did. I didn't know why exactly, but something in my gut told me this woman wasn't lying about the baby. It would be so easy to prove it wasn't mine, and she wouldn't be foolish enough to pull this over on me and think she could get away with it if it weren't true. But something in my gut also told me I wasn't getting the entire story. She was still holding back. She was still hiding something.

"But I also believe there is much more to you, and now is the time to come clean."

She paused for a moment but then continued on walking. "I haven't had the easiest life," she began. "In order to survive, I did some things that I'm not exactly proud of. I ran a lot of cons, and I deceived many people. I hustled and—"

"Was getting pregnant part of a con?" I interrupted. She wouldn't be the first person who trapped a rich man by getting knocked up. I thought it was a fair question to ask. Did she see me as an easy mark since I was getting shit-faced in a bar in an expensive suit?

"No," she answered softly. "The pregnancy was not planned. I wouldn't have had unprotected sex, just like you wouldn't have. I know that might be hard to believe—"

"I believe you," I stated again. I needed her to understand that fact. "But now we have to discuss what happens from here. We have another life to think of beside our own."

"I'm quite aware of that." She placed her hand on her stomach and, for the first time, I looked at her belly and truly realized there was a living being in there. A living being I helped create. I let the thought in. I let it sit.

And then the overwhelming need to do something, anything to try to make this all "right" nearly took my breath away.

"So first of all, we need to get you to see a doctor. I'll have Mrs. H sneak one in as soon as possible. And then we need to get those special vitamins I know pregnant women are supposed to take daily."

I glanced down at her stomach again. "We want the baby to be healthy. And then we need to get those baby books that tell us what to expect. Oh, and those pregnancy pants. I'll order some of those special clothes you'll need."

A list of To Do's were going off in my head like rapid machine gun bullets. "Maybe I can get a maternity yoga instructor here, and what about a breastfeeding expert? And do we need to talk about a midwife or regular doctor?"

Abilene laughed. "Slow down there!"

She stopped walking and turned to face me. "I understand you want to try to take control of the situation, but you're going too fast. We need to focus on the right now. All that other stuff you mentioned... well, why don't we focus on the Trials for now."

She had a really good point. "If the Elders find out you're pregnant, they'll disqualify us." We started walking slowly again. "And maybe they'd be right in doing so. Maybe it's not safe to have you do them any longer."

"I don't think having orgies is going to hurt the baby."

"It's more than just sex, and you know it."

"Nothing we've done up until now put the baby's life at risk even in the slightest or I wouldn't have done it. I didn't even drink the champagne if you remember," she pointed out. "Besides... we both need to complete the Trials. You know it as much as I do."

"True," I agreed. "I need to take over the business. Even more so now that I have a family to think of."

The sun was beginning to really heat up and my back, sticky with sweat, told me we needed to get inside where it was cooler. "Let's get you inside. It's getting too hot out here."

"I'm not fragile, you know. Just pregnant." But she turned with me and headed back to the manor.

"I get that. But we need to think about the baby's safety. And you are right that we need to continue on with the Trials... for now. Though, I'm telling you right now, that if I ever so much as think any harm will come to you or the baby, I'll stop everything immediately."

"I get that," she murmured.

"And I still want you on those vitamins, and I'm still getting those books. We need to come up with one of those birthing plans too. Oh, what about those labor classes where they teach us how you breathe and stuff? We have to plan for this." I needed to get back to the room so I could start listing everything down.

Abilene chuckled. "God forbid we don't plan on how we're going to breathe."

So Beau knew about the baby. My big, bad secret was out. And everything was... fine. Fine-ish?

I should've known he would just take it in stride and start planning everything to death. He'd mentioned the baby's *college fund* after we'd gotten back from breakfast this morning.

The kid wasn't even born yet, and he was thinking about where they'd go to college! Jesus, I could barely think about getting through next week.

But here was Beau, ready to storm the castle, plan everything from the kid's preschool to their ideal collegiate pedigree, and I was just... I was just...

I was overwhelmed. And a little terrified that Beau was doing exactly what I'd been afraid he would. He was making all these plans, but rarely was he checking in with me to see if it was what I wanted for my child.

He was a bulldozer in a china shop, and it was hard not to worry it would be a constant fight to keep my *own* place in my kid's life. He was a take-charge, take *over* kind of man.

It felt more important than ever to win the Trials and *demand* my place in my own child's life, as ridiculous as that might seem.

Even though Beau did always say *our* baby and *our* kid's education. I just... Everything felt even more uncertain now that I'd told him.

Which was why I didn't mind that a Trial Invitation came for that night. Beau immediately freaked out about what might be asked of us, especially since there wasn't anything telling in the box—it was empty, i.e., I was supposed to show up naked. Shocker.

But frankly, I was ready to show Beau that he didn't have to treat me like I was made of glass. Yeah, so it was sort of cute the way he kept checking to see if I had enough blankets at night and I was taking the vitamins he'd had Mrs. H smuggle me and how he put wet compresses on my head when I was sick in the mornings. No one had ever cared about me like that, actually.

Then I reminded myself it was just because he knew I was carrying his child. It wasn't about me at all. Which was fine. Really.

But all the books I'd read before coming here said I should be completely safe doing normal to vigorous physical activity. Pregnant women were not invalids, for Christ's sake. And tonight I'd show Beau that first hand.

Because one thing the books *hadn't* warned me about?

I was insanely horny. Like, ready to jump Beau in his sleep and bang his brains out horny.

But guess what Mr. Suddenly Over-Protective was suddenly loath to do?

That's right, *ding ding ding ding*. He hadn't *touched* me in the sexy times way since he'd found out I was pregnant. Mrs. H hadn't helped, coming over like she had when he'd been giving it to me *so damn good* during the last Trial. I could have wrung her neck. Him slapping my ass was not going to hurt the baby. Or him fucking me like the beast I loved him to be.

And to go from that animal sensuality to... *nada*. Dear Lord, my body was aching for him, especially since my libido was in overdrive like never before.

I hoped whatever the Trial was tonight required him to fuck my brains out. Repeatedly. Please, if there were a God!

I could tell by the stormy expression on Beau's face as he dressed up in his stiff tux and I stripped all the way down that he wasn't exactly feeling the same excitement for tonight's Trial.

"Loosen up," I said, leisurely unsnapping my bra and freeing my breasts right in front of him. "It's gonna be fine. We go down, we fuck, we come back up. Don't tell me you have performance anxiety all of a sudden."

Satisfyingly, he was distracted, his eyes zeroing in on my breasts before he dragged his eyes back up to my face, eyebrows pinching together. "You need to be taking this more seriously."

I laughed as I fluffed my hair out. "Oh, I'm taking it seriously." I turned toward the door. "I *seriously* need to get fucked," I muttered under my breath.

And then, within the space of a breath, Beau's hard body was up against my back, one hot hand on my waist. He spoke into my ear, his breath warm and tickling. "I mean it, Abilene. Be careful tonight. Don't antagonize any of the Elders. Just do exactly what they ask and no more."

His hand slid around from my bare hip to my stomach. "And if it's ever too much, you just say the word and it all stops."

I spun around to face him, my bare breasts smushing against his tux coat since we were so close. It felt incredible, and I fought to keep my focus.

"Let's keep one thing straight," I said. "I am not quitting. I need to know you'll be there to back me up and not pussy out on me. I need to know you can trust me and not be Mr. Macho Protector or you'll give away our secret and get us both disqualified. No matter what happens, keep your thoughts to yourself. You need to trust that I would never do anything to harm this baby. Can you do that?"

His jaw tensed and he looked like he wanted to argue. I knew he valued his control over all else, so I really did get what a big deal it was for him to finally eke out a, "*Fine*."

He took my arm as we headed downstairs. I don't think it was so much an act of chivalry as a need to hold on to me and the last bit of his control before we were subjected to whatever the Elders had in store for us.

There was no music tinkling up the stairs as we made our way down, and I tried to pretend the silence wasn't ill-omened.

So I guessed it wouldn't be a party/orgy atmosphere tonight?

Then we got into the white ballroom, and I immediately felt Beau tense beside me. All the Elders were there, in their silver robes and their ominous wooden canes, but there weren't the usual naked women spread around servicing various members.

No, tonight there were simply two little stations in the center of the room.

One was a chair with a small table where it looked like a man was setting up... was that *tattoo* equipment?

But it was the other piece of furniture that had my eyes popping.

It looked almost like a gynecological exam table, except all done up in leather. But there were absolutely stirrups that seemed meant to spread my legs wide open at an obscene angle, considering I was buck naked. There would be no part of me that was not on display.

Especially once I noticed that the stirrups had straps attached. I would be strapped to that thing, my legs held open.

Beau stepped forward, glaring everyone down. "This is not a white-collar situation. No one's cock goes in my belle except mine," he stated firmly.

One of the elders stepped forward. I blanched a little when I saw it was the man who'd roughly ordered me to massage his prostate at the last Trial and then become so quickly displeased when I wasn't doing it right. But seriously—who has *that much* experience sticking their fingers up a dude's ass and can find the prostate on the first try? Not me, obviously.

"You are an Initiate," the man declared loudly. "It is not for you to make demands. But tonight's Trial is merely the marking of the belle as belonging to the Order. You will be marked as well, as per tradition."

The way Beau's face suddenly went beet red, I thought he might be about to burst a blood vessel. Apparently, I wasn't the only one who saw, because another man stepped forward, much younger than the rest. And then I remembered Beau telling me about him—he was Beau's friend, Montgomery.

"And as traditions continue forth, we also acknowledge that some of the old ways must be adapted to more modern sensibilities," Montgomery said. He met Beau's eyes while he talked. Then he turned to the rest of the Elders and raised a flogger. "Which is why those who would be pleased to, may take their pleasure in flogging the belle on her inner thighs before the piercing of her flesh."

Oh shit. Flogging? Piercing my flesh?

If I thought Beau was tense before, it was nothing to the concrete pillar he'd become beside me at this pronouncement.

But there wasn't much time to over-contemplate things, because then Elders came, put hands on Beau, and pulled him away from me toward the tattoo station.

And similarly, Elders came forward and pushed me toward the spread-eagle medical chair.

Beau's head spun to look over his shoulder. His gaze caught mine and I saw it in his eyes. He was about two point three seconds from calling the whole thing off. From announcing I was pregnant and blowing both of our chances.

I glared him down and shook my head. I could handle this. I *would* handle this. By God, I would.

But even as determined and stubborn as I was, I couldn't say my limbs weren't still shaking as I climbed onto the strange piece of furniture.

Foreign hands were all over me. Stroking down my legs as they lifted each into position in each stirrup. Squeezing as they pulled the leather straps tight around my calves and shins. A squeeze of my breast here and fingers trailing up my inner thighs there.

But they kept to their word and no one unbuckled their belts or came toward me with their cock out.

I let out a deep breath I hadn't even realized I'd been holding.

You can do this, I coached myself. *No biggie. You got this.*

But then the canes began to pound the floor, one of the most terrifying sounds in the world as it echoed back and forth around the huge, otherwise empty room.

I felt like the proverbial ritualistic sacrifice being offered up to the gods, spread out and spread-eagled like I was, tied down and completely vulnerable.

I heard the buzz of the tattoo gun as it started up and my eyes flew over to Beau. They'd set up the two stations, so we had a perfect vantage point of the other. Probably part of the point, I imagined. For each of us to see the other as we endured... all that they had in store for us.

I was still looking at Beau when the first blow hit.

The *snap* of the leather flogger fringe against my inner thigh had me yelping and sitting up as far as I could while being strapped down to the chair. It wasn't far, because they'd strapped my torso down as well.

"That's pretty, turn those thighs a pretty pink," the first Elder crooned as he worked the flogger back and forth in an X pattern on my thighs.

Only to pass the flogger off to the man who'd lined up behind him. He didn't strike so much as massage my now pink thighs with the flogger. Then, before I'd quite recovered from the repeated stinging slaps, he reached down to pinch the flesh of my inner thigh, *just* a finger's length away from my sex.

The next two men were very concentrated with the flogger, and I braced for every blow, the inside of my thighs on fire.

I was shaking from sensation and pain, and when I lifted my face, unbidden tears spilling down my cheeks, I saw Beau watching. They had his wrist, and the tattoo artist was working away but Beau looked like he was ready to leap out of the chair and come rip me out of mine.

I shook my head at him and then closed my eyes, sinking back onto the leather and trying to give myself over to the process.

The next man wasn't interested in the flogger at all. He just rubbed his calloused hands up and down my sore inner thighs, which were now shaking uncontrollably. He pulled them apart, stretching me even further open.

"What a pretty pink pussy," he said. "Take a look at this pink, pink pussy. That's right. Stretch it wide. Wider. Come on." He pulled at the flesh of my thighs and indeed, I could feel my sex being opened wide for the view of all in the room.

Murmurs went through the room.

"Get her clit nice and big for the piercing, Brian," called out the first Elder.

Oh shit, it was my *clit* they were going to pierce? I guess it was obvious now that I looked down and saw my position.

The man between my legs, Brian, I supposed, was only too happy to oblige the request made of him. He wasn't an unattractive man. Maybe in his mid-forties. An excited glint entered his eyes as he sucked on his finger and then reached down to place his fingers on my sex.

My whole body jolted at the contact and I couldn't help it, my eyes sought out Beau. The vein at his neck bulged as the other man began to play with me, fingering my folds and finally locating my clitoris.

I blinked back tears of emotion as first his finger began to circle it, then another man came up to replace him and another hand was at my sex.

Somebody squirted lube on me and then there were multiple hands, multiple men. Pulling at my pussy, stretching me wide. Rubbing me.

And goddammit, I was only human. My body responded. I was on a knife's edge, all my hormones cranked up to a ten.

My pussy softened and flushed and expanded under all the ministrations. My clit grew and pulsed.

Occasionally, a flogging of my inner thighs would bring a shock of pain to break through the confusing mix of pleasure and sensation that had my entire body shaking.

And then the hands would be back, big male hands, probing and pulling at me, and rubbing, always rubbing and circling and teasing until I could barely stand it anymore.

I kept my eyes locked on Beau, feeling tortured by pleasure but also like I was betraying him. This wasn't what I'd wanted for tonight. I'd wanted *his* body. *His* hands.

And instead, I was being caressed and rubbed and teased and oh God, oh *God*—

"Come," Beau called out. "Fucking come for me, belle. Scream for me while you do it."

The second he gave permission, I wailed, and my breasts arched as much as they could with the restraints. The orgasm that had been building for the last twenty minutes tore through my body.

Hands were everywhere on my body. I closed my eyes and imagined they were Beau's hands. His hands rubbing me, touching me in my most intimate places, teasing at my asshole as he commanded me so gruffly to *come*.

"Beau!" I shouted as I came, and came, and fucking *came*. Someone shoved their finger up my asshole, and I wiggled on it, shamelessly thrusting my hips as others continued, hands working my pussy and clit.

And then they'd released Beau and he rushed toward me, shoving his pants down as he came.

Oh thank God, oh thank God. I wept with relief.

All the other men scattered as he wasted no time stepping between my absurdly spread-eagled legs, grabbed my still-stinging thighs in an unforgiving grip, and shoved himself all the way to the hilt deep inside me.

I cried out and thrust back against him as much as I was able, but he held me down with his hands, moving them to my hips. He held me ruthlessly to the table and fucked me, his eyes dark, menacing, and full of a dangerous lust.

But for the first time since he'd learned about the pregnancy, thank fuck, he was not being gentle with me.

I came against almost instantly, so riled up from the torturous play with my clit that I was already on the edge within seconds.

I squeezed around his cock as I convulsed, and we locked eyes as he shoved deep inside me again and growled, then pulled back one last time and shoved inside again so roughly, the whole damn table moved backwards with the force.

He roared as he came and I clenched and welcomed his cum into my body, spasming even harder around him.

"And now we mark her as the Order's," came a voice from behind Beau. Beau clenched his teeth, and for a second, I thought he would snarl his refusal. But he didn't. He pulled out of me, a rush of cum pouring out with the movement. I arched up, already missing his weight the second he was gone.

But before I could do or think anything else, the man who'd tattooed Beau was coming forward.

I blinked and laid my head back, not sure I could watch this part. I hadn't had anything except my ears pierced, and that was when I was fourteen and Tina had the great idea to do it with ice cubes and a needle. It had hurt like a bitch, but we'd done it.

So I braced myself, shocked again when hands touched me in my intimate place. But the hands were gloved this time, more clinical. Still, my clit was huge and swollen, and every touch felt sensitive and made me quake.

He washed the area and, far before I was ready, I felt pain lance through my center as he pierced me.

I screamed for holy God, the pain of the flogging seeming like child's play compared to the piercing.

But then the man had backed away and I looked down, barely able to catch my breath I was breathing so hard.

A little ring with a glittering diamond stud on it now twinkled from my clitoris.

No doubt a Radcliffe diamond.

Marked again as *his*.

" $\Large{A}$ re you sure you're okay?" I asked, cradling her in my arms as I rushed back to the room.

"I told you I'm fine. The baby's fine."

"We don't know that," I said, pissed at myself that I allowed those fuckers to flog her inner thighs and pierce her damn clit!

And what did I do? I fucked her. I couldn't help myself. I had to be inside her. I had to have her. But the baby...

"I do," she reassured as she held on tighter around my neck when I fiddled with the door handle to our room. "The baby is perfectly fine."

When I placed her on the bed, I pointed my finger at her and ordered, "Don't move. I'll be right back."

I rushed to the bathroom and ran a washcloth under warm water. I nearly ran back to the bed where, luckily, Abilene had actually listened to me and remained propped up against the pillows. She had a warm smile on her face and shook her head as I approached.

"I'm okay, really."

"Spread your legs," I ordered, not satisfied with her answer. I wanted to make sure no skin on her thighs was broken, that there wasn't any bruising, and that the idiot limp dicks weren't too heavy handed with the flogger.

With a sigh, she did so and allowed me to run the cloth over the red and inflamed inner skin. I tried not to focus on her jeweled clit, and I most definitely tried to not pay any attention to the fact that my cock was getting rock hard again. Something about this woman turned me into an animal with primal urges and an almost feral desire to throw caution and reason out the door if it meant I could be buried balls deep inside of her.

Clearly. Her pregnant self was proof of that.

There was a small knock on the door with Mrs. H walking in. "I brought a special ointment for the piercing," she said. "We want to make sure we keep it clean and cared for."

"It's coming out the minute we leave this place," I said, not stopping with wiping the washcloth over every inch of flogged flesh.

"Hey there," Abilene said, snapping her head off the pillow and glaring at me. "I may want to keep it. I might like it."

"It's coming out," I said again, and I meant it.

"All right, well," Mrs. H said as she approached the bed, determined to break up any impending fight. "No need to discuss the matter now. Let's just focus on what's in front of us." She handed the jar of ointment to Abilene. "Twice a day." She then looked at me. "It wouldn't hurt for you to use it as well on your tattoo for a couple of days. Keep it moist so it doesn't scab over."

"What's your tattoo anyway?" Abilene asked. "I never got to really see."

"Two sabers crossed," I mumbled, not really seeing it as a big deal.

Growing up knowing it was a tattoo I'd eventually get sort of took the shock value out of it. However, I was extremely grateful that the Elders had modified the tradition of the belle also getting the mark of the sabers—because instead of just a tattoo, the belles used to get it *branded* into their skin. I seriously doubted I would have allowed any man to get anywhere near Abilene with a hot poker.

"I want you to get a doctor here immediately," I said, finally done with cleaning between Abilene's thighs. "I want to hear the baby's heartbeat. I want to know that everything is all right, and the baby is in no danger at all."

"It's not that easy," Mrs. H said. "I've been working on it since the last time you asked. We can't use the Oleander doctor because he'll tell the Elders. Hell... I can't use a doctor within a hundred-mile radius of Darlington County because it will somehow get back to the Elders. I'm trying to find someone who is so far removed from any of the members of the Order and that's no easy task."

"Get Montgomery or even my dad involved if you need to. I trust them to keep it discreet," I offered.

Mrs. H nodded. "I'll find someone. But in the meantime, you need to rest easy that everything is fine. Abilene is in perfect health, there's no spotting or cramping, and women function normally throughout their entire pregnancy with no issues. She doesn't need to be babied."

"You know I'm right here," she said, waving her hands at the both of us. "You are both speaking like I'm not lying here in this bed... naked... I might add. May I have some freakin' clothes please?"

She moved to get out of bed, but I quickly placed my hand on her leg and gave her a warning glare that was enough for her to freeze and settle back in like I had expected.

I quickly went to the dresser, pulling out a tank top and shorts I had known her to wear for bed.

"I know you both have a lot on your plate right now," Mrs. H said. "And I want you to know your secret is safe with me. But I also have to warn you that the Elders have a way of knowing everything that happens in this manor. The Oleander has eyes in the walls."

"We'll be careful," I said, helping Abilene get dressed whether she liked it or not.

"They won't let Abilene continue if they find out," Mrs. H reminded.

"We know," I said.

Abilene slapped my hands when I tried to help put her shorts on. "I can do this myself," she bit out. "Jesus, I'm not an invalid."

Mrs. H chuckled. "Girl, you better get used to this. I know Beau, and when this man gets focused on something, he doesn't let go. I can clearly see his laser focus is centered on you."

I chose to ignore the rolling of Abilene's eyes and instead said to Mrs. H, "I want us to start discussing the menu. I don't want to overstep, but I've been reading about certain foods that are rich with the vitamins needed for the baby. And I'm a bit concerned Abilene isn't maintaining a healthy weight. It says in the book a woman should gain—"

"We are not going to discuss my weight!" Abilene interrupted.

"You're underweight," I said, giving her another warning look. "And calm down. Getting stressed isn't good for the baby."

"First of all," she said as she took a deep breath. "I'm not underweight. We also don't want me putting on pounds while I have to be buck ass naked in front of everyone for the Trials. Second of all, it is not *me* who needs to calm down. You're wired so tightly right now that I keep waiting to see your head pop off."

Rather than arguing with her, I redirected my attention to Mrs. H. "Can you also do me a favor? I want to start getting my place baby-proofed. I don't even know where to begin or who to call on this. Is there a way you can help me out?"

"Beau!" Abilene said as she leaned forward and took a hold of my forearm. "I understand you are a natural-born planner. I appreciate that you want the best for this baby. But you're really starting to freak me the fuck out."

Mrs. H stepped forward and patted my back. "I agree with the lass. You need to relax. You getting all worked up isn't going to be good for you, Abilene, or even the baby. Don't worry. I'll work on the doctor. I'll also help with the safety of the house if it makes you feel better. But right now, you need to focus on finishing this Initiation. You both need to really concentrate on what still lies ahead for you." Mrs. H then looked at Abilene. "Can I get you anything?"

Abilene shook her head. "No, thank you. I think I have *plenty*," she paused to glare at me, "right here."

With a final chuckle and another pat on the back, Mrs. H left us alone.

I made eye contact with Abilene then and hardened my expression. "I want you to be honest with me. Do you really feel like the baby is okay? This isn't a time to be tough or to try to *protect* my feelings. I want the truth."

She sat up and took hold of my hand. "I would never let anything bad happen to our child. You need to have faith in that. Everything is okay. I promise."

Satisfied with her answer and finding comfort in the soothing way she delivered the message that I needed to chill the fuck out, I stood and reached for the blankets to tuck her into bed.

"It's been a long night," I said. "I'm sure you need your rest."

"Wait." She didn't release my hand. "Can you... come be with me? I could really use..." She swallowed hard, her eyes diverted, but then refocused on me. "Could you hold me until I fall asleep? Please?"

I don't think I could have stripped down and crawled into bed fast enough. I needed to hold her and was happy she also wanted that. I didn't want to push too fast or too hard even though I really couldn't help myself in that matter. But I needed to hold her.

And as I took her into my arms and rested my hand on her belly... I realized I needed to hold the baby too. It was all truly sinking in. I was going to be a father.

Abilene pressed her body into me in the perfect spoon. "We're going to be all right," she said softly. "We're so close to the end. I'm sure we only have a couple of Trials to go, and this will all be over. We can walk out of here with everything we both ever wanted."

I took a deep breath and inhaled the flowery essence of her hair. My dick was hard because it had a mind of its own, but I had no true desire to fuck her. I just wanted to hold her, hold my baby, and be as one.

"Beau?" she asked sleepily with a yawn.

"Yes?" I kissed her head and squeezed her to me even more. I had this overwhelming need to protect and didn't want her even an inch away from me.

"My life has always involved lies. I want to change that. I don't want to lie again. I don't want this baby to have to hustle. I want so much more for them."

I kissed her head again. "I know. And don't worry. I believe you about the baby. The baby *will* have the best. Never doubt that. We don't need to discuss this any further."

"I know you say that, and I know you think you—"

"Shh," I interrupted. "You need your rest. We both do. I think we've talked enough for one night. Sleep."

She released a breath and placed her palm over mine that rested on her stomach.

No more words.

Just us. Just the three of us.

T hings settled into a bit of a rhythm over the next few weeks. Beau worked and I read books and watched old movies on the TV Mrs. H got me at Beau's request. I loved the glamour of old Hollywood and could lose long afternoons watching Gene Kelly movies. I'd also watched almost the entire Hitchcock catalogue.

"What do you even like about these old movies?" Beau asked as he closed his laptop at the end of another endless day.

I looked up from where I'd been laid out on the floor on my side, eating popcorn and laughing my ass off at one of the amazing singing and dance numbers in *Singin' in the Rain*.

I grabbed the remote and rewound. "Are you kidding? Watch this. Donald O'Connor does a running wall flip. No special effects, he's just a badass."

I played the movie forward, laughing in astonishment when the young Donald O'Connor pulled off the amazing feat, running at the wall and then flipping over with the ease of any modern parkour star.

I grinned as I looked from the screen back to Beau. "Badass, right?"

There was a smile on his face, but he wasn't looking at the screen. "Badass indeed," he said quietly.

I swallowed and sat up from my laid out stance on the plush floor rug. "So, um." I licked my fingertips free of salty butter, a movement which did not go unnoticed by Beau. His eyes zeroed in on my lips as I licked each finger.

Oh shit, that was hot. I pulled my last finger from my mouth with a little *pop* and felt my cheeks heat.

I looked Beau up and down. Everything had been so different the past few weeks. He'd been so... attentive. I imagined he was driving Mrs. H nuts with his insistence on overhauling the menu, but she'd risen to the task. She made me green smoothies for breakfast every morning, and just this past week the nausea had been slowly settling down.

But the weeks before that, Beau wouldn't let me just hide out in the bathroom during the nauseous mornings anymore.

No, he insisted I keep the door open, and he'd come in and check on me. On really bad mornings, he'd stay beside me while I wallowed by the porcelain throne. He'd hold my hair back, rub my back, and help me into the shower after my stomach finally settled to get cleaned up.

He made sure there were always crackers by my bedside and that I ate some before I ever got out of bed. One of the many things he'd read in the pregnancy books—which he'd read cover to cover. I was almost certain that he was now more prepared for this baby than *I* was. Which was only slightly disconcerting, considering that sometimes it still felt completely unreal to me.

I mean, I couldn't actually be about to have a *baby* in six months. That was ridiculous. Absolutely freaking bonkers.

Except that Mrs. H had come through after all. She'd found a doctor to come visit on the down-low.

It was a former belle, who Mrs. H believed could be trusted to keep our secret. The Order had no more sway over the former belle because her dream had been to be put through medical school. Well, the woman was a doctor now in Atlanta, and when Mrs. H had explained my situation, the woman had felt compassionate enough to agree to see me. Especially when Mrs. H explained that Beau would pay handsomely for her services.

So last week she'd arrived and been discretely smuggled into our room by Mrs. H. My belly was still flat. The only change I'd noticed in my body was that my breasts were getting a little heavier, especially now that Beau and Mrs. H were on a two-person team ganged up to get as much food down my throat as possible every day.

I couldn't say I wasn't anxious as the woman pulled out her portable ultrasound and plugged it all in. Then she turned on her laptop, squirted some cold gel on my tummy, and started to push her ultrasound wand against my stomach.

At first there was just silence, and I'd never felt more terror than I did in that moment of horrible, abject quiet.

But the next moment, there it was. *Wom-wom-wom-wom-wom-wom-wom*. The baby's little heartbeat so rapid and absolutely rock steady.

Beau was standing right beside the bed where I was lying, and his hand had shot forward and grasped on to mine. I'd gripped back to his hand just as tightly.

Listening to that heartbeat made my entire world shift.

Yeah, I'd known there was a baby. But there was something different about knowing and *hearing evidence* of their freaking *heartbeat*.

Then, in addition to having our hands locked, I'd looked up and my gaze hit Beau's and it was like *pow*. Not only was I having a baby. *We* were having a *family*.

A thought that freaked me out so bad, I tried to pull my hand back from Beau's. But he wouldn't let go. So I stopped fighting him.

We hadn't talked about where *we* stood in light of this big bombshell I'd landed right in our laps. We hadn't talked about where that put the two of *us* in terms of his all-important contract.

Did he still consider me just... contractually? Had anything changed for him?

I felt like an idiot in that moment. Thinking about romance, feeling insecure about how a man may or may not feel about me when I was hearing my baby's heartbeat for the first time. But it wasn't like these were exactly normal circumstances. How the hell was I *supposed* to be feeling? There wasn't any template on how to do this.

And thankfully, the doctor broke into my thoughts before I could spiral down the looking glass too far.

"Everything looks great. You're about twelve, thirteen weeks along, yes?"

I nodded.

"The baby was conceived on Friday, May 1st," Beau said. "Does that match what you're seeing?"

Well, that was a splash of cold water on all my fanciful angst-filled thoughts. He was checking with the doctor to see if I was lying about him being the father. To double-check the timing of the pregnancy?

The doctor laughed. "It's rare a patient knows the exact specifics, but yes, May first." She paused and looked toward the ceiling like she was double-checking her calculations. "That matches perfectly."

She looked down at her watch. "So you're twelve weeks almost to the day." She went on to explain what I could expect as I entered the second trimester.

Beau proceeded to pummel her with question after question about my health. Gestational diabetes, his concerns about my continued nausea and whether or not I was getting enough caloric intake each day, even what was the best *brand* of prenatal vitamins.

She patiently answered all his questions, then looked back to me. "Now, are there any other questions *you* have, mama-to-be?"

It was probably stupid to ask just how much it would hurt to give birth to the baby, huh? But as if she'd read my mind, she asked, "Have you started thinking about a birthing plan? It's a little early, but sometimes planning can be a way to help ease any pre-baby jitters."

But before I could get a word out, Beau jumped in with, "What about physical activity?" He furrowed his eyebrows at the woman. "You know exactly what goes on here. Is it safe for my child if she continues with the Trials?"

The woman didn't give us a quick answer, which I imagined Beau preferred. I did too, if I was honest. While I might not be at a Beau level of paranoia, I was still concerned.

The Trials the last few weeks had all been benign —along the lines of group orgies where all the Elders could get their wicks waxed by some pretty woman or another.

One time more collars showed up in a box, but there was a black one this time, which meant I could stay at Beau's side.

The Trials were the only time Beau had sex with me.

He was so careful with me the rest of the time, sometimes I wondered if he was attracted to me anymore at all. If I'd just become the sexless mother of his child.

At least until a Trial came.

Maybe it was just his need to fully and enthusiastically participate while all the Elders were watching on?

I had no clue, but the things he did to my body when we were both on display for all to see... dear *God*. I got the voracious lover back my body was craving more and more. The times in between the Trials started to feel cruel.

I'd sit all day in the same room with Beau, my body on fire with the longing to touch him, to rub against him, to fucking *ride* him...

But no. I had to just stay at a distance because of... well because we hadn't discussed whatever the hell we *were* to one another now, and I was afraid if I asked, he'd bring up that damn contact again, and then I'd have to strangle him with it!

Apparently, Beau had finished interrogating the doctor, because she was finally packing up her equipment.

"I'll be back in three weeks and we can find out the sex of the baby if you'd like."

"No," I said, at the same time as Beau said, "Yes."

We looked at each other and his face immediately darkened. "Abilene. We want to know the sex of the baby."

That commanding, demanding tone of his was so damn sexy, and also absolutely infuriating. "Do we? I think it's more fun if it's a surprise when I give birth."

He shook his head. "That's ludicrous. We can purchase appropriate clothing and decide on a name if we know the sex of the child."

"Oh really?" I took the paper towel the doctor gave me and wiped at the leftover gel on my stomach before sitting up. "Says who? *You*? Look, buddy, times have changed since your old Boys Club days when they founded this place. It doesn't matter if it's a boy or a girl. I'm not into painting the bedroom pink if it's a girl or blue if it's a boy. Gender is a construct and—"

"So are you suggesting we name the child Apple? Or perhaps Rocket?"

I rolled my eyes at him. "I suppose you want Beau Jr.?"

The way he shrugged told me he had totally considered it. "Oh my gosh, you've got to be kidding me. I'm not naming my son after you! If it's a boy, that is!"

He crossed his arms over his chest. "Why not? It's my firstborn too."

I glared at him. "Well, come up with some different name options, buddy. Because I veto Beau Jr."

That had begun what I—on my more generous days—referred to as the Great Name Debate. On my less generous days I referred to it as the Shut the Fuck Up We're Naming the Kid What I Want to Name Them.

Which had continued for the last week and a half.

I grinned up at Beau from the floor now as *Singin' in the Rain* continued playing in the background. "How about Gene if it's a boy?"

"Like Simmons? No thank you."

"No, like Kelly. Don't you want our little love muffin to be debonair?"

"Hard pass."

I rolled my eyes and reached my hands up. Beau took my hands and pulled, helping me up off the floor. I tried (and failed) to ignore the zing of electricity that raced through my body at even the brief contact of his skin on mine.

Was I absolutely shameless in finding excuses to touch him? Yes. Yes, I was.

Did I feel bad about it? No. No, I did not.

"If it's a girl," he said, "how about—"

But whatever he was going to say was cut off by a knock at the door.

Our eyes locked, and then Beau walked swiftly to the door and opened it.

"Your presence is requested at a Trial in one hour sharp," came Mrs. H's voice from beyond the door. I couldn't see her because Beau's big body was blocking the way. When he turned around, she was already gone, but he was holding a white box in his hands.

My heartbeat started fluttering. And not in fear of whatever might be in store at the Trial.

No, my heart started racing because a Trial likely meant I'd finally get to sleep with Beau again. My sex contracted even at the thought of having him deep inside me once again.

Beau was busy ripping open the box. He frowned down at it, then he turned it toward me. It was completely empty.

I shrugged. "So they want me naked. That's nothing new."

Beau nodded, looking away from me and swallowing. "Yes. I'm sure it will be fine."

Was he thinking about it too? How he'd fuck me tonight? Or was he worrying about the baby, because that's all he thought of me as now—just as an incubator?

"I'll let you shower first," he said, turning so that his back was to me.

Infuriating man.

I stomped past him and turned the shower on hot. If only I could wash this man right outta my hair.

I could tell tonight was going to suck simply by looking at the faces of my friends, Montgomery and Rafe. They were in their new silver robes, and their eyes revealed all I needed to know.

Abilene and I were fucked.

We were in the ballroom again, which was a room I had grown to detest since being an Initiate. Oh, how times had changed from the days of being a young boy playing in this room and not being able to wait until the day I was old enough to be a member just like my good ol' dad.

My good ol' dad who avoided eye contact with me when I entered the room with a nude Abilene by my side.

There was a reason why my father wasn't an Elder. I never knew what that was or why he never tried for the position. My father did not lack ambition, actually quite the opposite. So, there must have been another reason.

Maybe tonight would give me a peek as to exactly why. Maybe he chose his path and becoming an Elder was just too dark of a trail to walk for him.

The room was empty tonight. Free from naked women and horny men. Tonight was going to focus on Abilene and me only. The members and the Elders were the only ones present... unless you counted the Devil.

The Devil was most certainly present. I could feel him.

There was a very large contraption in the center of the room. It was a glass container about six feet high and wide enough to fit a person inside. No doubt Abilene or I would be that person. On top of the glass box was a black container that covered the top and went all the way to the ceiling. My guess was something was inside the upper half and would be dropping its contents down on whoever stood in the clear box.

I didn't have much time to really process what was about to occur because the Elders began pounding their canes against the white marble floor. Beat after beat, their cadence being the only hollow and deafening sound in the elegant room.

Members flanked behind Abilene and me, and an Elder moved forward and took Abilene by the arm. He led her to the glass box and shoved her inside, closing the door loudly. My heart nearly stopped, watching her stand with her arms by her sides, awaiting what was next.

She had such pride and strength. Her head was held high, and if she was afraid, she didn't show it in the slightest. If anything, she had an expression on her face that screamed: *Give me the best you've got, motherfuckers.*

Naked or not, the woman didn't appear vulnerable in the slightest. She was prepared for battle, and I had never been more impressed with another human being in my life as I was with her. She glanced up above her for any sign as to what would come, but we both had no idea what would be dropped upon her.

The canes continued to beat, and as they did, other Elders emerged with silver rope in their hands. They began wrapping the glass box in the ropes, tying knots as they went.

They were trapping Abilene in the box with the knotted ropes.

Slowly and methodically the glass box morphed into silver. A silver serpent nearly swallowed Abilene whole.

Deep in my bones, I knew this wasn't going to be good. I could see that the only way of getting Abilene out of the box was by undoing everything the Elders had just done. Every knot, every twisted weaving of the rope would have to be untied to free her.

And the entire time I helplessly watched the woman who was carrying my child slowly disappear behind the rope, I wanted to scream. I wanted to demand for this to be over. I was so fucking tired. I was so damn exhausted fighting the moral battle within. This was wrong. What kind of man allowed this? What kind of man would risk a woman and his baby? For what? Money? A business? Pride? Blueblood heritage laced with sin? What kind of man was I?

It didn't matter how many damn baby books I read. The one thing I did know was that it was my duty to do whatever I had to do to protect the mother of my child. And as she stood in a glass box, surrounded in knots of silver, I realized I was slowly failing her... one Trial at a time.

"Beau Radcliffe," an Elder said, breaking me from my thoughts. "It is your duty to free your belle. Save her, and you complete the Trial. Failure to do so means..." His voice trailed off as the sounds of the canes intensified.

Means what?

What?

I had heard rumors of past belles and women who had accidents at the Oleander. Tales of nameless graves in the graveyard up the hill. Missing girls no one really cared about. Secrets never to be spoken. Ghosts of belles walked the grounds due to Trials gone wrong. But were they just rumors? Were they just ghost stories to scare boys like me growing up? Or were they truths?

Jesus Fucking Christ. Was Abilene's life in danger?

Not wasting another second, I charged to the glass box and began tugging at the rope. I could quickly see that I had to be smart about undoing the knots.

Pulling and using brute strength was only tightening them.

"It's okay," I heard come from the other side of the glass. "You got this, Beau. Stay calm. Don't let this rattle you."

I could see enough of Abilene between the rope, and I knew she could see peeks of me, but there were so many knots getting in the way of us.

An Elder called out, "Allow the Radcliffe riches to rain down on the belle."

The black box above her opened and a small stream of clear glass marbles mixed with diamonds began to rain down upon her.

And there it was. The worst Trial yet.

I needed to free my belle or she would be suffocated by my family's diamonds. The Radcliffe jewels would destroy her unless I could somehow unleash these binds.

Nothing would stop me. Nothing.

I started one knot at a time, trying to ignore that Abilene was buried up to her ankles already. "Are you doing okay in there?" I asked as I pulled and maneuvered the rope.

"Focus, Beau. I'm fine. I'm fine."

"There's so many fucking knots." I undid one only to reach for another. And another and another.

"You can do this. Don't quit this Trial. Don't let them win. Don't let this Trial be the one that makes us fail. Whatever you do, don't quit. Promise me."

I couldn't promise her that. No way would I allow this to go too far. If the diamonds and marbles got too close to her face, all bets were off. But for now, I worked frantically at the knots with every intention of freeing her.

But the rain of sparkling hell fell fast, and her body was slowly being covered. Knot after knot, I made some progress. I could see her face now. I could see her eyes, and though she was covered up to her waist, she revealed no fear. Her calm soothed me and allowed me to fight on. My fingers bled from the skin being rubbed raw. My fingernails were pulling up as I refused to let the Elders beat me with their handiwork.

When the diamonds and marbles covered her belly fully and reached her breasts, I panicked. There were still so many knots, and the glass box was filling up quicker than I could undo them.

Pools of rope coiled at my feet, and yet it felt like I wasn't getting anywhere.

Abilene reached out her hand and placed her palm against the glass. I looked up from a bloody knot and made eye contact with her.

"I'm trying, Abilene. I'm fucking trying."

"You got this. I trust you. I know you can do this."

"Is the weight too much on you? Tell me. Is it too much? Can you breathe?" I could only imagine how suffocated and claustrophobic Abilene must feel.

"It's fine. I'm fine. Keep going." Her eyes went to the remaining knots and, for the first time, I saw a flicker of fear in her eyes.

She saw what I saw. The speed of the box being filled was beating my own speed with untying the knots. The diamonds were winning.

There had to be another way. I wouldn't be able to do this in time. There had to be another way.

Fuck the Elders.

They had no rules for this Trial. There was only one goal.

Free the belle.

Well, I planned to.

Running to the side of the room where a chair sat, I picked it up and ran back to the box.

"Cover your face!" I shouted as I slammed the chair into the glass, expecting to see the glass shatter all around.

Abilene shielded her face with her arms, and as the chair made contact with the glass, the only thing that happened was the leg of the chair broke off.

The glass box remained intact.

I tried again with more force, roaring in frustration.

The glass box mocked me with its reinforced strength.

This wasn't normal glass. It was shatterproof.

The Elders had expected my reaction and planned accordingly.

The canes began to beat against the floor again, as if they were laughing at my actions.

The glass marbles were up to her collarbone by now and a horrific terror nearly took me down at the knees. The knots were still there, and I had only wasted time with my barbaric act of thinking I could just bulldoze my way through.

I ran back to the knots and began frantically pulling at them. I looked at Abilene who had tilted her head back in preparation to keep her face uncovered as long as possible.

"Can you climb up at all?" I asked.

"No, I can't move. Just hurry," she said, her voice coming out weak and ragged.

I looked at Montgomery and Rafe. "Help me! Get her out of there. Nothing in the rules say you can't help. Fucking help me!"

What surprised me was that the first one to move toward me was my father. He ran toward the box and began working at one of the knots. Montgomery and Rafe quickly followed. I waited to hear the Elders call out foul or announce the Trial was over due to disqualification, but I didn't care. I wanted Abilene free at whatever costs.

And as the diamonds circled around Abilene's face, the four of us worked frantically at the knots, and I saw a light at the end of the tunnel. We were so close.

So close.

But in another couple of minutes, she wouldn't be able to breathe at all.

Fuck me. Fuck me.

The woman I loved was about to die right before my eyes. She would be one of the belles victim to a Trial. Not a rumor. Not a ghost story. A true story, a tragedy I'd let happen.

She would walk these halls in forever damnation because once the Oleander had you, it never let go. Abilene and baby Radcliffe howling for release for eternity.

"Get her out of there!" I screamed.

"Only a couple more knots," my father said. He looked up from his knot to Abilene who was taking shallow breaths as diamonds trickled down upon her. She spit them out of her mouth and sucked in air. "Hold on a couple more minutes, beautiful. We'll get you out. I give you my word."

The one thing about my father was he was a man of his word. He never broke a contract, never promised and under delivered. So with his words to Abilene, I attacked my final knot with renewed vengeance. I was so focused on my task that I ignored that the fingernail of my index finger popped off.

The burning pain told me one thing... We were close. So close.

And just as she took one last deep breath, the marbles and diamonds covered her face completely.

Please don't let it be her last dying breath.

"Faster," I screamed. "She's completely covered! She can't breathe. Get her out!"

Finally, we unfastened the only remaining rope. I yanked it off and opened the box.

The marbles and diamonds rushed out of the box like a tidal wave of sin. They covered the floor of the ballroom as I reached for Abilene's body and pulled her to me. She gasped for air as she clung to me for strength.

"It's okay," I soothed as I ran my hand over the back of her head, holding her against my chest. "I got you. I got you and I'm never letting you go again."

Tears of relief fell from my eyes and my heart beat so hard it physically hurt. I didn't care what anyone thought, or what the consequences were going to be for me asking and taking help from others.

"I knew you could do it," she said, shaking as she still held tight to me. "I never doubted you. I knew you wouldn't let us down."

"Never again," I said as I kissed the top of her head. "Never will I ever fear losing you again. Never."

The pounding of the canes began again. Not stopping, not turning, I ignored the sinister sound.

"Beau Radcliffe," an Elder said from behind me. "You have completed the Trial and saved the belle. You relied on the power of the brotherhood of The Order of the Silver Ghost as a member will be expected to do. The evening is complete."

17

I was still shaking by the time Beau got me back upstairs. As soon as he shut the bedroom door behind us, my hands went to my stomach.

"Are you okay? Is the baby okay?" He immediately began bombarding me with questions.

I held up a hand. "I'm fine. I'm fine. I just..." A shudder ran through my body. "I just need a minute."

On trembling legs, I made my way to the bed and collapsed down on it.

Beau was immediately at my side, and then his hands were on my body, running up and down my arms, on my stomach, even checking my pulse until I finally shoved him off.

"I said I'm fine!" I shouted.

"Well, forgive me but I just watched you get all but crushed by fucking marbles and goddamned diamonds!"

He stood up and paced back and forth, dragging his hands through his hair. Completely opposite of the stoic, put-together Beau I was used to. It was just as bizarre as seeing him lose it downstairs when he started picking up furniture and frantically bashing it against the glass to get me out had been.

I took a deep breath. "They didn't crush me. It was horrible. I won't say it wasn't horrible. I couldn't move and there was pressure on all sides pushing in on me and, yes, I started to panic. But just because it felt like I was going to die, I don't think I actually would have. It was just an absolutely horrible, torturous thing to do to somebody. Like being buried alive, and they made you watch."

Another shudder wracked its way through my body and Beau stopped pacing, coming back to my side and putting his arms around me. This time not diagnostically. He just held me. He held me until the trembling slowed.

"I'm so sorry I couldn't get to you faster," he whispered, and I could hear the anguish in his voice. "I should have done better. If I could have just stayed calm. Or stopped the Trial. You should *never* have been put in that position in the first place—"

I shook out of his hold so that I could look at his face. "When are you going to get it? This isn't something that's all on you. We're in this together. You did amazing. Way better than anyone could have expected. And you got me out. I was right to trust that you could."

He started to shake his head, but I grabbed his hand. "Hey. Listen to me. You're going to make a great father."

He froze at that, and I could tell my words hit him deep, because he swallowed hard. He was silent a moment, and then he asked, "What if I fuck everything up? What if I screw the kid up beyond all repair?"

I laughed at that. "I'm pretty sure every prospective parent is afraid of that. At least the good ones. You think I'm not afraid of that too? I want so much for this kid." My hands drifted back to my stomach, and again I blinked at the thought of the little creature growing there and the potential life ahead of them. "I want so much that I didn't have," I whispered.

Then my eyes came back to Beau. "Why do you think I did this crazy thing, coming and tracking you down like this? I'm not perfect, obviously, but I'm fierce in wanting the best for this child."

Beau smiled and reached out a hand. At first, he hesitated, and then he ever-so-gently pushed a lock of hair behind my ear.

I melted into the brush of his fingertips against my cheek.

"Yes, fierce is the right word for you," he said. He left his hand where it was, cupping my cheek, his eyes piercing mine. "I like what you said about doing this together. Even downstairs, your voice was the only thing keeping me even marginally sane. You're an amazing woman. What if we..." His voice trailed off and his eyebrows narrowed as if he was thinking deeply about something.

But then the muscles in his forehead eased, as if he'd made some sort of decision. "Maybe we could give this a go in the real world. I'll do everything in my power to give this baby the best life." His hand on my cheek flexed ever so slightly. "And to give *you* the best life."

My breath caught at his words. "Are you— Do you mean—" But I couldn't quite finish the thought. It was too fantastic. Too good to be true. Was he saying he'd actually consider *being* with me?

"I never had a traditional family growing up," he said.

I shook my head. "I didn't either."

"I was so terrified down there. I couldn't protect you, and it fucking *killed* me—"

"But you *did* protect me," I said in a rush. "You saved me. And we're so close to the end. It's just another month now. Less than a month." And now he was saying that after that month, that we could — That we could really try this... I sucked in a deep breath, still not able to fully let myself believe it.

He moved closer into me, so that our thighs were smushed against one another, but I wanted him closer still. When he took my hand, I immediately interlocked our fingers. The energy between us was electric, and I felt fevered.

"It could be our chance," he said, "to have it all. The family neither of us had before. We could make it, together."

"I want that," I whispered, as I leaned into him, intoxicated by his nearness.

And he met me. Dear God, did he meet me.

His lips crashed down on mine and then he was all but pulling me into his lap.

I was still naked, and he was still clothed, but the thread count of his tux was so high that my naked sex against the crotch of his pants felt heavenly. The piercing in my clit had healed and even the slightest friction had me tingling.

Especially when I felt the bulge of his need thrusting up from underneath the fabric. My sex contracted at the feel, and I threw my arms around his neck.

We hadn't had sex in almost a week since the last Trial and my pussy was weeping with need for him. I'm sure I'd already left a spot on his pants.

"I need you inside me," I breathed into his ear. "Please, Beau. After tonight, I need the connection."

He groaned and flipped us so that my back was on the bed. Moments later, he'd shucked his pants and boxers and then he was above me. I spread my legs to receive him and then he was there.

He sank inside me in one, not gentle thrust.

And I loved that. I loved so much that he wasn't treating me like a porcelain doll. He grabbed my hip, and I wrapped my legs around his hips, jerking upwards when he next thrust in, meeting him so that our bodies slapped together in an erotic noise.

He massaged my hip in his fingers. I moaned and again met his next thrust.

"More," I begged. "I need to feel you everywhere."

"Goddammit, woman," he growled.

And then he'd pulled out and he was manhandling my body in the way that I absolutely loved. He flipped me and demanded, "Hands and knees."

I scrambled into position, and then he was behind me, sinking gloriously into me again.

I wiggled my ass at him, gripping the sheets and mattress and shoving back against him as hard as I could. Then I reached back with one hand and spread my ass as wide as I could, which elicited a low, growled, "*fuck*," from him that had my sex clenching around him as he next thrust in.

I wiggled again, and he got what I was asking for without words.

He smacked my ass, another glorious sound echoing through the room.

"Again," I begged, and he did. Over and over he spanked my ass while he fucked me from behind.

And his cock banged that spot so perfect inside me with every thrust and I rocked back against him as the best kind of tremors began—the release of tension, of the night, of everything that wasn't Beau and me.

But right as I began to come, he pulled out again, leaving me whining with unrealized release.

He rolled me again, so I was on my back and then he lowered his body between my legs. He entered and was fucking me again, his chest lowered to mine, those piercing, intense eyes looking right into mine.

My breath caught and the orgasm picked right back up where it had left off. I reached up and grasped his face, kissed him, and came so hard it felt like I escaped my body. Except no, I'd never felt so at one with my body, every nerve ending lighting up, feeling so connected with Beau inside me, Beau on top of me, Beau's lips, Beau's eyes, Beau's *being*.

And when I felt the hot rush of him spilling deep inside of me, my body clenched one more time before exploding in an even brighter wave of light.

I was terrified in the same moment, because after having this, how could anything—anyone—ever compare or measure up? And I was also terrified that Beau would go away and turn cold the moment he pulled out, like he had last time we'd connected so deeply.

But he didn't. Instead, afterwards, he pulled me tight into him, little spoon to his big, and we fell asleep with his arm curved protectively around me.

I'd never felt safer or more wanted a night to never end.

18

BEAU

Working from a bedroom was becoming almost impossible. I had tried my best to return all messages and to take as many phone calls as I could, but one of my strengths in business was how I handled people. I could read people like a book, and I had a look that told them not to mess with me.

It was much harder to negotiate or discipline from afar. It was challenging to instill the fear of God into someone by words only. I needed to be present. I needed my life back. And I needed to feel some level of control in this new chaos I lived in.

It had been two weeks since the glass box Trial with no further communication from the Elders. Part of me was grateful that there hadn't been any more Trials, but another part of me grew more and more anxious as each day passed.

Why hadn't we heard from them?

Had they found out about the baby?

Were they planning on kicking us out on our asses... as failures?

Or were they simply busy? I did know that both Walker and Emmett still had their Initiations coming, and maybe it was as simple as the Order being preoccupied with preparing for the other initiates.

Closing my laptop, feeling like I had worked enough for one day, I focused my attention on Abilene who was lying on the floor doing sit-ups.

"What in the hell are you doing?" I asked both amused and slightly concerned that crunching her belly repeatedly wasn't good for the baby.

"I'm getting fluffy," she answered, winded.

I got up off the chair, bent down, grabbed her by the arm and lifted her up to standing. "You've lost your mind. There isn't anything *fluffy* about you." I kissed the tip of her nose to try to hide my smile.

She raised her shirt and pinched the flesh of her belly. "I'm starting to show. The Elders will be able to figure it out soon unless I do something."

Looking at her belly, which may have a slight rounding to it if anything, I said, "If they notice anything at all, it's that you and I *both* have put on a little weight. We can blame good cooking and inactivity." I patted my belly for emphasis. "We can both be *fluffy*."

Rolling her eyes, she sat back down on the floor to resume her exercise. "You are far from fluffy, Mr. Six Pack."

Taking her by the arm again, I warned, "Don't make me show you what I do to stubborn girls who don't listen."

She smirked and licked her lips. "Oh really?"

My cock twitched at all the dirty thoughts running through my head. "Really. Don't make me punish you."

She leaned back on her elbows and looked up at me. "Maybe I can't help it. Maybe I'm just a naughty girl."

Her tease was so fucking hot. My cock didn't just twitch this time but instead hardened to full attention.

Dropping to my knees, I took hold of her body and flipped her onto her stomach. Without hesitation, I yanked her cotton shorts and panties down to her knees, completely baring her firm ass. I moved so quickly and effortlessly that Abilene didn't even have time to protest in the slightest. It wasn't until I spanked her ass that she released her first squeal.

"Don't say I didn't warn you," I said as I began to pepper her ass with one swat after the other. I held her down and trapped her legs with the weight of my own.

She was helpless to my wicked ways.

"I'm going to spank every inch of your ass until you scream out my name, and only then will I stop so that I can claim this ass as mine."

Her gasp was all I needed to know that she wasn't going to argue against my plan.

My next swat was much harder than the last few, and then Abilene suddenly jerked against me and shouted, "Oh my God!"

When I lifted my weight off of her, she instantly sat up and held her stomach wide-eyed.

My heart lurched as panic took over. "The baby? Did I hurt the baby?" I didn't think I was being too rough with her, but clearly I was the idiot who thought I could be kinky with a pregnant woman. "Do we need to get to the hospital?"

I knew that Mrs. H was arriving soon with the doctor to do an exam and ultrasound, but maybe we needed to act immediately.

She shook her head frantically, with her hand still on her belly. "No, no. The baby." She looked at me with tears in her eyes and a smile ghosting her face. "I felt the baby kick!"

"It moved?" I placed my hand on her belly in hopes that I would feel it, too, but didn't feel anything but her hand which she placed over mine.

We both sat in silence waiting for the baby to move again.

"The baby is stubborn like you," she said, still smiling bigger than I'd ever seen her do. "Plus, I think it's too early for you to feel from the outside."

"If the baby's stubborn, they got that from *you*."

There was a knock on the door followed by Mrs. H popping her head inside. "You ready for the doc?"

I nodded. "Come on in."

We realized that Abilene still had her pants pulled down, so we were both scrambling to get them pulled up before the doctor entered. I then helped Abilene off the floor and led her to the bed by the hand. Mrs. H and the doctor entered the room, rolling the ultrasound with them.

"How's Mama feeling today?" the doctor asked.

"She felt the baby kick," I answered for her. "Is that normal for this stage of the pregnancy?"

The doctor gave me a little smile and then looked back at Abilene. "It's normal. Especially if you're in tune with your baby."

The looks the three women in the room gave me told me that I needed to stop trying to take over and relax. I wasn't blind, nor was I dumb. I knew I could be an overbearing asshole, but I couldn't help it. Although I did go up to Abilene's side and hold her hand as the doctor began the examination. I would try to be good and remain quiet. I would try...

"Everything looks great, and the baby looks perfectly healthy." She moved the ultrasound wand across Abilene's belly and asked, "Do you want to know the sex?"

"Yes," I answered immediately.

Abilene looked up at me and then the doctor. "You can see it?"

The doctor nodded.

Abilene then looked back at me. "You really want to know?"

At that very moment, I had never wanted anything more. "I really do. But this isn't just my choice. It's ours."

Abilene squeezed my hand and then nodded at the doctor. "We want to know."

"Congratulations, Mom and Dad. You're going to have a baby boy."

A boy. A Radcliffe boy.

"Oh my God," Abilene said under her breath. Her hand squeezed even tighter.

A son.

I was going to have a son.

And a family.

A rush of emotions and thoughts gripped my heart like a vise. My life was about to change. Everything I had planned for and expected had just been altered. Reality sunk in. No more holidays alone. No more Christmas nights spent having dinner with my father and no one else.

No. I wanted more for my son. I wanted a family tree that we decorate together. I'd never had a tree that was mine, full of ornaments that held special memories or homemade by me at school. I didn't bake cookies for Santa or write a letter of all the gifts I hoped to get.

No. I just got an envelope of money every year when at this very moment I swore to myself my son would never receive that as a gift from me. Never. He'd get a bike, and a wagon, and a swing set—all that I built myself.

And it wouldn't be just me and my son sipping bourbon by the fire. It would be the three of us. I saw Abilene in my future too. I knew she'd be a good mother. That fighting spirit in her would do good for my son. He'd grow up with two powerful parents who would raise him to be a fighter and yet a good person. Yes, my boy would be a good person who took others' feelings in consideration before his own. He would get the best of me and the best of Abilene.

"We're having a boy," Abilene said to me, breaking me out of my thoughts. "Is that what you were hoping for?"

"I didn't have a preference... or at least I didn't think so." But now that I knew the sex of the baby. "Yes, I'm so happy we're having a boy."

I blinked away the tears and leaned down and kissed the top of her head.

"All looks completely fine. I don't think you need to see me again until after the Initiation is over," the doctor said as she began packing up. "Mrs. H has my contact information if you want to reach out to me afterwards, but once you leave here, you'll want to get a closer doctor and set up a birthing plan." She smiled at me and then Abilene. "Congratulations."

"This doesn't seem real," Abilene said as she sat up and wiped at her stomach.

"Oh, it's real," Mrs. H said with a joyful laugh. "A mini Beau Radcliffe... Lord help us all." She turned on her heels still laughing and exited the room.

"A Radcliffe," I repeated. "I never thought I'd carry on the family name."

I looked down at Abilene who had tears cascading down her face. I swiped at a tear with my thumb and then cupped her chin so she had to look into my eyes.

"I will always be there for you and our son. Always. I give you my word. And in my world, our word is everything." I swallowed against the emotion that nearly choked me. "You and this baby will be my everything."

I was going to have a baby. A little baby boy.

I was going to have *Beau's* little baby boy.

The days were long and unending... and yet part of me never wanted them to end. Especially with the long stretch of time with no Trials, it was just me and Beau secluded away from the world.

He worked, yes, but not from dawn to dusk like he used to.

He took extensive breaks for breakfast, lunch, and dinner and we'd talk and tell stories and make each other laugh. He had a wicked humor underneath that dry, no-nonsense demeanor. He told me endless stories about the shit he and his friends used to get up to, as kids and then as teenagers at Darlington Prep.

It was a world I couldn't imagine, except I could, because it came so alive through his eyes and words as he shared it.

I was more mum about my past. I still didn't know how to share who I'd been when I wasn't exactly proud of everything I'd done. It still seemed a little too close to the surface to talk about my former career scamming guys. My justifications that the only dudes I scammed were assholes rang a little hollow now.

It wasn't the person I wanted to be anymore. It wasn't the kind of mother I wanted for my son. I wanted to make an honest living, even if I tried to understand that my options had been limited at the time that Tina had taken me under her manipulative wing.

The future would be different, though, and that was all that mattered. At least that was what I told myself when the old anxieties came back.

Everything just seemed too good to be true. How could I trust this? How could I truly trust Beau?

He said he wanted to be there for me. Not just the baby, but for *me*. He said he wanted a future with me once we left the Oleander... but there had never been mentions of any specifics.

It was easy to wonder if they were just words said in the heat of passion. When the going got tough... would he get going? Would he leave me in the dust like every single person had before him?

When he wrapped his arms around me at night, usually after yet another exhaustive bout of lovemaking, it was easy to believe his words. His promises. It was easy to believe that a happily ever after could be possible. Even for a girl like me, who'd been thrown away like trash her entire life.

But then morning would come, and the bed beside me would be cold and empty. Beau always woke up before me and he'd be away at his desk, answering emails before breakfast.

I told myself it was silly. I was being overly needy and hormonal. I refused to be clingy and beg him to come back into bed. I would *not* be that woman. I wouldn't make him pay for the sins others had committed against me in my past.

And yet the wounds that I'd thought long scabbed over felt torn open again and regularly salted until I felt like a neurotic mess. Likely it was just the damn pregnancy hormones. It was like being on a damn rollercoaster of emotions, though, and I did *not* fucking appreciate it!

I wanted to be fun and easy-going and attractive. Not a bloated, occasionally sobby mess. Everything I'd ever wanted but never truly dreamt I could ever have was within my reach and I was terrified I'd somehow blow it without even meaning to.

But then there was Beau. With a touch, he could ground me again. Or make me laugh. And I'd come back to the present moment and be pulled out of my stupid brain cycling over every terrible scenario and for a moment, or an hour, feel at peace.

We were just finishing up one of those luxurious lunches—where Beau sternly eyed me until I finished my entire Cobb salad. Dark leafy greens, broccoli, and eggs were all big on the Pregnancy Diet plan he and Mrs. H had cooked up. I went along with it, as long as I was able to slather on liberal amounts of bacon ranch dressing. It was delicious, and Beau was trying to coax me into eating more blueberries—high in antioxidants— when Mrs. H came in with a big white box.

I pulled back from Beau trying to shove a blueberry in my mouth to look at Mrs. H. Then I looked to Beau. His face had gone pale. It had been so long since we'd had a Trial, and the last one had been so traumatic, I think more on him than on me, in the end.

"It'll be fine," I said, reaching across the table and grabbing his hand. "Just think of it as a chance to slap my ass in public."

Mrs. H didn't say anything, she just set the box on the table, then turned around and left again.

Beau frowned. "Was that ominous? She didn't say a thing."

I shook my head and whispered, "Shhh. She's just always conscious there might be other ears around."

He nodded, then slid the box closer and lifted the lid. His eyebrows drew together and now he looked really worried.

"What is it?" I asked.

He pulled out a long, silk, dark red robe.

I reached out and touched the soft, silky fabric. It slipped right through my fingers. "Sexy." The robe even had a little hood on it.

"Maybe it's a Red Riding Hood kink?" I suggested.

Beau nodded but didn't look convinced. He grabbed his glass of lemonade and swigged it like it was bourbon before saying he needed to get back to work and that we should head back to the room.

He was on edge for the rest of the day. I watched more old movies to pass the time and tried to zone out. Beau was just being over-protective like always. I was choosing to consider the fact that they'd actually given me any clothing at all this time as a good thing.

Even if, after I'd showered and gotten ready for the evening, then stripped down and put on the sheer robe, it all but felt as if I was wearing nothing at all anyway.

The material fell down my back in a sheer rush of silken fabric. But the front of the robe... well, that was a different story. The silk did nothing to hide my peaked nipples. Instead, it accentuated them, almost to a pornographic extent. If it really was a Red Riding Hood kink, they'd hit the nail on the head.

Beau was silent and brooding as he got dressed.

I squeezed his hand as we got ready to go downstairs. "Hey. We got this. There's nothing to be scared of. I got your back and you got mine, yeah?"

He let out a loud rush of air before nodding firmly. He lifted our clasped hands and kissed the back of mine. "Yes. Always."

And then downstairs we went.

I was hoping for an orgy situation. Sure, some bastards might try to cop a feel, but I knew Beau would be his normal protective self and keep me safe.

When we walked into the white ballroom, however, I realized there would be no such luck.

I gulped when I saw a large, clear water tank with a stool set up precariously over top it.

I'd seen something like it before at a fair.

It was a dunk tank.

Unlike at the fair, there was no target set up to throw a ball at in order to dunk the person sitting on the stool. I knew without the Elders saying a word that I'd be the one sitting on that damn stool.

The clingy red silk robe made a little more sense. I was sure I would look fabulously sensuous soaked with it stuck to my body like a sheer second skin. I might as well be naked. No doubt it was something these fuckers would get off on.

Beau's hand tensed on my arm as he escorted me into the room.

I pulled away from him and squared my shoulders.

It might be an uncomfortable evening, but there wasn't a seal on the top of the tank, and it was at most three feet deep. I wouldn't drown. I'd just likely feel like a shivering, drowned rat.

Before I had much more time to consider what the evening ahead might hold, those goddamned canes began pounding the floor, a sonorous drumbeat as an Elder came forward and pulled me away from Beau.

He grabbed my forearm and yanked me forward, none too gently. I could all but feel Beau's bristling anger behind me at the Elder's rough treatment. I looked back at him over my shoulder and narrowed my eyes at him.

We hadn't specifically talked about it, but he better remember all I'd told him about trusting me to know what I could and could not handle.

His teeth clenched and his jaw flexed, but he stayed still. Good boy.

"Climb to the seat of judgment," the Elder manhandling me demanded once we got close to the dunk tank.

Somehow, I didn't think saying, *um, hard pass*, would go over very well. No, I had to be the dutiful little woman and voluntarily climb to whatever punishment or *judgment* they'd decided in their deluded minds I was due.

So I grabbed hold of the rungs of the ladder on the side of the tank and started climbing. It was awkward once I got to the top to straddle and hold on to the stubby back of the stool to get my ass onto the seat, but I managed.

I was barely seated before one of the Elders in his gleaming silver robes stepped forward and all but yelled, "Confess, harlot!"

My mouth dropped open; I couldn't help it.

But then the other Elders and members all around the room took up the call, banging their canes as they chanted, "*Con*-fess, *con*-fess, *con*-fess, *con*-fess."

My eyes flew to Beau, but then I yanked them away again. Shit. They knew about the baby? Oh shit.

I didn't want to incriminate Beau, so I kept my eyes off of him, but even in the brief moment of eye-contact, I'd seen that he was completely freaked out too.

The first Elder held up a hand and the chanting died down. He eyed me with a cold stare. "Will you confess?"

I slowly shook my head. "I don't understand. What do you want me to—"

But I wasn't able to finish my sentence. The Elder ever-so-slightly nodded his head, looking somewhere past me, and the next thing I knew, the stool underneath me was dropping away.

"Wait!" I yelped, but obviously it was too late.

My screech was cut off as I dunked underneath the cold water. Jesus Christ, cold. Cold, cold, cold!

I scrambled and got my feet underneath me, then stood up, gasping and spitting water. As expected, my scarlet robe clung to my body. I covered my shivering arms across my chest. Screw them. They were going to put me through this, they didn't deserve a peep show on top of it.

"Climb back to your seat," the Elder demanded, unmoved by my shivering, water-logged self. Hell, maybe he got off on it. You never knew with these bastards.

Gritting my teeth, I climbed the secondary ladder that was on the *inside* of the tank, and again performed the mini-gymnastic feat to get back on the stool. The chill air of the air-conditioned space made chill bumps pop up all over my arms and entire body. I tried not to give them the satisfaction of shivering but couldn't help still holding my arms across my chest. I knew it was a defensive posture, but I didn't know what human wouldn't be on the defense with a roomful of hostile-looking men glaring at her and shouting at her to *confess*, whatever that meant.

"Confess where you went to high school, Abilene West. Confess the name of your favorite high school teacher."

Oh shit.

Was this not about the baby at all?

Beau stepped forward. "I don't see what this has to do with—"

"Confess!" the examiner demanded, and again, everyone around the room took up the chant, "*Con*-fess, *con*-fess, *con*-fess."

I opened my mouth. "I don't remember high school. Who can remember their high school—"

The water rushed up to meet me and smacked me in the face, flying up my nose. I splashed to the surface spitting and flailing. Fucking *bastards!*

"Why so hesitant, Ms. West?" asked the examiner. "These are simple questions."

"Maybe I would answer," I snarled. "If you'd stop dunking me in freezing water every three seconds, and I could have a moment to fucking *think*!"

Silence in the room, and I knew, shit, I'd gone too far. They valued delicate little Southern roses here. Wilting roses without any thorns.

"Back on the chair," snapped the Elder.

Two red blotches appeared high in the man's cheeks. I was not making him happy. At least that meant he wasn't getting off on this.

I spit out another mouthful of water I'd gagged on, right in his direction, then I went back to climbing.

It went on like that for ten more minutes. The Elder asking me details about Abilene's life that only she would know, and unhappy with my vague, palm-reader type answers.

After asking where Abilene lived now, I answered, "Well, right now I live here, obviously. The Oleander Manor. Afterwards, I'll likely find another apartment. It seemed silly to pay rent on an apartment since I'd have all expenses covered while I was here."

There. Nice and tidy and it gave nothing away.

Apparently, the Elders thought so, too, because next thing I knew—

DUNKED.

I came up sputtering. "What do you *want* from me?" I all but yelled in frustration, forgetting my promise to myself to stay cool for Beau's sake. I'd been keeping my eyes firmly averted from him but in that moment, I broke and looked his direction. He looked tortured, absolutely agonized by what was happening to me. But we both knew he couldn't do anything. Moreover, I'd *asked* him not to intervene, and for once he was respecting that, no matter how much he *wanted* to.

But if there was a sweet moment between us, it was gone in the blink of an instant when the thunderous canes started up again.

Feeling like my body weighed three times what it normally did, I dragged my sodden form up those stupid ladder stairs yet again.

How long could they keep this up? Considering they weren't the ones getting dunked in the cold water... probably a while.

So I was both surprised and relieved in a twisted way when they just cut to the chase and asked, "Where is the real Abilene West?" as soon as I'd reseated myself on the stool again. Even though I knew it meant I was found out, that everything was lost, and that so much of what I'd fought for might be entirely lost.

They didn't wait for me to answer. As soon as the question was out of the Elder's mouth, they dunked me again.

As I hit the water, I realized that this wasn't a real inquisition. This was all meant as a macabre sort of punishment. I'd wounded their pride by sneaking so easily into their world, into their twisted game that they thought they owned the rules to and control over.

And they wanted to punish me for breaking those arbitrary rules.

I finally found my footing and stood up tall. I whipped my hair back and forth and squared my shoulders, unashamed in my scarlet robe that did nothing to hide my nakedness.

And I looked that accusing Elder in the eye as I answered him: "I have no idea where Abilene West is. My name is Consuela Borden, and I took Abilene's invitation as my own."

It was only out of the corner of my eye that I saw Beau stagger several steps backward, and it was in that moment that I realized I'd lost it all. I'd been *thiiiiiiiis* close to everything I'd ever wanted. And I'd been fool enough to think I could even have it. But life was doing what life always did—snatching everything good away right at the last second. Nothing ever changed for girls like me.

My own mother didn't love me enough to stay around. Why did I think anyone else would fight for me?

I climbed the ladder out of the dunk tank, slung a wet leg over the other side, then slung my other one over the top and jumped the few feet to the polished wooden floors of the ballroom. I landed with a *thud,* but the Elder was apparently no longer concerned with me. He'd turned back to the crowd at large.

"The harlot has confessed! Initiate," the Elder skewered Beau with his glare. "Did you know of the harlot's deception?"

Beau just shook his head, looking dumbfounded. "I didn't know she wasn't Abilene," he said. He didn't look my direction, and that burned.

"Then you are banished to the foyer while we decide your fate," the Elder declared dramatically.

A punch to the gut would give me the same effect. I wheezed for air as I spun around to face her. "What the hell is going on?" My voice boomed off the walls of the foyer.

"I was going to tell you," Abilene—Consuela— whatever the fuck her name was, said.

She was shivering and dripping, and a part of me wanted to give her my jacket, and another part of me wanted to see her suffer.

"When?" I asked. "Once you popped out my baby?" I looked at her belly. "Is that baby even mine? Is that another lie?"

"Don't ask that," she snapped. "Everything I've told you is the truth! The truth."

"Except your damn name!" I took a few steps away from her because I felt as if she was suffocating me with her very presence. "Who the fuck are you?"

"Simple answer? A con artist," she said softly. "Or at least I used to be. And I *told* you that. I didn't hide anything. I hustled to survive. One mark after the other. It was my life. It's all I ever knew. And when I saw my chance at getting in the Oleander... I made it mine."

She took a step toward me, crossing her arms to try to conceal her nudity beneath the sheer robe. "When I found out I was pregnant with your baby, and then you told me all about your Initiation, well... I saw an opportunity."

"An opportunity to con me?"

"I didn't con *you*," she said quickly. "I mean, yes, I lied about my name but that's it. I took an invite from a belle who didn't want it. I had to pretend to be her to be given a chance. But I didn't con you. Not you."

I huffed. "That's how this looks right now."

"Which I understand. And trust me, this isn't how I wanted you to find out. I thought I could keep the secret until we were at least out of this place."

"I want the truth," I turned to face her head on. "Is that baby mine?"

She nodded as she said, "I swear to you, it is. I would never lie about that. I would never lie to my baby about who his father is. And I know deep down you believe me on this."

"I want to believe. I always have. But then I also believed you to be Abilene West, so, clearly, I'm not as good a judge of character as I thought. I was an easy mark, right?"

"You were never my mark. When we hooked up at the bar, I didn't know who you were or even planned on having sex. Sex has never been part of my cons. I never went there. You and I were simply two people who had intense chemistry, too many drinks, and..." She took a long inhale and then added, "The Order was my mark. Not you."

"Why?" I asked. "Why do all this? Who would want to go through all these Trials? You were already pregnant with my baby. Payday was coming your way already. So why?"

"Because I needed to do what was best for the baby. I couldn't care for a child with the type of life I was leading. I wanted the money so that I would be able to raise my child with everything I didn't have. But I also wanted—"

"Did you think I'd be a deadbeat dad?" I interrupted. "Did you think I wouldn't support the baby?"

She took a deep breath and calmly said, "I wasn't going to be at your mercy. I knew you were a powerful man, and it scared me. Money buys decisions in your favor, and a part of me worried you'd take the baby. No, don't scoff at me. You could've crucified me in court, and I would *not* let you take away my child."

She paced in front of me. "Plus, I didn't want just the money. I wanted my baby to have a *name*. I refused for my child to be a bastard. And when I found out who you were, I wanted the Radcliffe name for my baby more than I ever wanted anything in my life. I didn't want *your* money. I wanted my *own* money, but I also wanted my baby to belong. So, yes, coming here and being chosen as a belle would give me money, and that's great." She looked at me, her eyes entreating. "But I wanted so much more. I wanted the baby to truly have *you*. Not just a paycheck from an absentee father."

"I would never be that." The very thought insulted me.

"How was I supposed to know that?" she asked, throwing her hands in the air. "I didn't know anything about you, not really. All I knew was that I had to try. I had to fight to be a belle. It could be life-changing, and it was. When you found out I was pregnant, you actually wanted this baby. You wanted a family. You even wanted me."

"Yes, but it was based all on a lie. Why wouldn't you tell me?"

"I tried," she said. "A couple of times. I wanted to, but at the same time you were starting to open up to me, and I was getting to see you for who you really were. I wanted to see *you*. The real you. I was scared that if I admitted my full story, you would close up. I didn't want to miss the opportunity of seeing you without walls. I was so scared of losing everything that you were giving. You were offering me and the baby a future which is all I ever wanted. You were giving me hope, and I was terrified that with my confession, it would all disappear." She looked down at her feet and then back up to my eyes. "I was falling in love with you. I was scared. I was scared I'd lose it all."

"And how am I to believe you now?" I asked, narrowing my eyes and trying to picture her as Consuela instead of Abilene. "How do I know you aren't just scamming me again?"

"You don't," she admitted. "And I understand if you can never trust me again. But I love you, Beau. I love this baby. And I love what the three of us could have. The only thing I lied to you about was my name. The rest was all me."

Love.

Did I love her?

Yes, of course I did. I fell in love with Abilene and the baby and...

Abilene, Consuela, Abilene...

My fucking mind spun, and heart twisted in a knot. I didn't know what to think or say. This entire situation was fucked.

I glanced at the door leading to the ballroom. "You know you could have fucked this all up for the both of us. Your lie could have not only cost you your payday, but also my family business. You could have ruined the Radcliffe heritage that you claim you wanted so badly for the baby."

She hung her head in shame. "I know. I was hoping they wouldn't find out."

"The Elders find everything out. These men are some of the most powerful men in the world. You picked the wrong mark."

"I have no excuses for you other than I did what I felt I had to."

"We're almost done. The final hour, and now it could all be ruined."

She nodded and took another step toward me. Her teeth were chattering, and no matter how mad I was, I couldn't just stand there and allow her to freeze. I reached out and took off the soaking red robe and then removed my jacket.

"Wear this," I said as I covered her body with my dry clothing.

"I'm sorry," she said, and something in the way she said it made me believe her. "If I could fix this, I would." She put her hand on her belly and added, "Everything I do is for this baby. Our baby."

"And what do we do now? Where do we go from here?" I asked.

"None of this changes the fact that we have a baby coming."

The door to the ballroom opened and Montgomery walked out into the foyer. I couldn't exactly read his face, but my gut told me he didn't have good news.

"How bad is it?" I asked.

"Bad," Montgomery answered. "Rafe and I tried to fight for you both. But we're new members. Our say doesn't go far."

"So are we fucked?" I asked.

"They're ready to see you," Montgomery said. "That's all I can tell you."

I clutched Beau's jacket around myself as if it were an anchor to safety, to him, to everything that had happened before this wretched night.

But as we walked back into the room of stern-faced Elders, I knew no jacket could shield me from their wrath or judgment.

"The Elders have come to a judgment in the matter of the Initiate and the harlot belle," declared the Elder who'd presided over my "confessional" earlier.

He stepped forward and banged his cane on the floor. I felt Beau stiffen beside me and didn't miss the way he sucked in a breath of air, tense and waiting for their decision. I squeezed my eyes shut, unable to watch. Dear God, I'd never considered that my deceit could cost *him* his inheritance. I'd never be able to forgive myself if he lost everything because of me. I'd just rushed headlong forward, panicked about the pregnancy, terrified of the child growing up the way I did, feeling unwanted or unloved, cast out by even one of their parents and determined to do everything I could to control an uncontrollable situation—

"The harlot belle is to be expelled with nothing. Her deceit and treachery will have no reward from this sacred and honored Society."

All around the room, canes banged the floor in solidarity with the judgment.

There it was, the official failure of all I'd hoped for.

I opened my eyes but kept them cast down to the floor. Beau went even more tense beside me.

The noise of the canes finally died down and the Elder's voice came booming out again. "We further declare the Initiation complete at no fault of the Initiate himself. We believe that no son of the Order would be complicit in such a deception and that Beau indeed did not know. Thus, Beau Radcliff, you have passed the Trials of Initiation. We welcome you to the brotherhood of the Order of the Silver Ghost. Come forth to receive your robes."

Beau stepped forward as canes banged the floor, leaving me all alone, shivering, naked except for his jacket.

I turned and immediately fled the room, the thunder of the canes echoing behind me. That was it, I was officially *out of here*.

I was a harlot? Screw all of them. I ran upstairs but then realized I didn't really have any "things" to gather. I changed into some decent clothes, the ones I'd brought in a small bag when I'd come. Everything else was clothing that was provided. There was nothing else to pack or take.

I took the back stairs down to the kitchen. Where I ran into Mrs. Hawthorne.

"I need my phone," I said to her. "Give it to me."

She frowned. "You can't just leave. You need to speak with Beau. Make things right."

I scoffed. "Look, I'm outta here. He had a chance to stand up for me. He didn't." I knew it was irrational as soon as it came out of my mouth. Beau had his whole future on the line back in that room, and I was the one who'd put him in that position. Still, this was all too much.

And it wasn't like in the foyer he'd said he loved me back after I stupidly opened my big mouth and confessed my feelings like a big idiot—

"Just give me my phone! I need to get the hell out of here!"

My nose was stinging and that meant tears were just seconds from following.

Mrs. Hawthorne frowned in disapproval, but she did disappear into the pantry and came back out with my phone. Jesus, it was hiding there the whole time?

"You should really wait and talk to—" she started.

I snatched it out of her hand and all but ran for the side exit I knew was off the small hallway out back of the kitchen.

As soon as I hit the hot, humid air of the Georgian summer, I felt like I could breathe. Except as soon as I sucked in a big breath, I was sobbing.

I started running. I needed to get away from the Oleander. I needed to put as much distance as I could between me and that fucking nightmare of a place.

Except even as I had the thought, I knew it was a lie. Because really what I was running away from were the wonderful memories with Beau. All the nights he'd held me close, his arm wrapped around me, his hand brushing my stomach. The way he'd whisper in my ear and tease me about what we might name our child.

How he'd caress me, and those caresses would turn more intense until we were making furious love in the middle of the night. How safe I felt in his arms, safer than I'd ever felt at any point in my entire life.

But then his face at the end flashed through my mind. How he'd looked at me like he didn't even know me. Asking if the baby was even *his*. How could he ask me that? After everything we'd been through? It was just a stupid name! I'd told him more about my past than I'd ever shared with anyone. I'd shared myself, my body, my innermost thoughts and dreams and hopes and—

I ran harder, as if the more distance I put between me and the Oleander, between me and *him*, the less it would hurt.

God, I'd been so stupid. Why was I even still thinking about him?

He didn't want me.

Of course he didn't.

I'd been through this before.

Finding my mother's cold, lifeless body as a child. Wanting her to wake up, but of course she never would. She'd left me behind because I wasn't worth staying for.

Tina leaving me in the dust when something better came along.

"It's just you and me, baby," I gasped through hiccuping sobs, finally slowing down and bending over, sucking in gulps of air by the side of the road. Towering oak trees swayed overhead, lining both sides of the road. Wind sang through the leaves, rustling and making sunshine dance around me in mockery of my pain.

I swiped at my eyes with my forearm. God, I was being ridiculous. I'd picked myself up before from devastating losses and I would this time too. I pulled my phone out and turned it on. Except of course the battery was dead after three months, so I couldn't even order an Uber, just my fucking luck.

"What the hell do you think you're doing out here?"

I spun around in shock at Beau's voice to see him jogging up from the road behind me.

My mouth dropped open before I waved an arm. "I'm leaving. What does it look like?"

He looked at me, bewildered. "What the fuck, Ab — Whatever your name is."

I glared at him. Anger was easier than hurt in this moment. "Consuela."

"Fine. Consuela. What do you think you're doing out here, in this heat? It's not safe for the baby."

Ah. Of course. "I'll be fine, thanks. I've been taking care of myself for a surprisingly long time before you came along."

"You weren't carrying my baby before."

I spun on him and shoved my finger in his face. "You don't get to be a controlling asshole just because you put a kid in me. I'll text you the address where you can send child-support."

Then I turned and started stomping back down the road, away from him.

To the surprise of absolutely no one, he followed. "What the hell, Ab— Consuela."

"It's Connie. I go by Connie, okay? Something you'd know if you remembered anything about the first night we met."

"Jesus Christ would you just stop stomping away from me and let me talk?"

I huffed out a furious breath and stopped, turning back toward him and crossing my arms over my chest. "Fine. Talk."

"God, woman. You are so damn *stubborn*."

I lifted an eyebrow as if to say, *yeah, and?*

"And I fucking love you."

I shook my head even as my chest seized up. "Stop it."

He looked flabbergasted. "Stop what?"

"Don't say shit you don't mean."

His face gentled and he took a step forward. "But I do mean it. I'm going to give that baby the Radcliffe name, but that's not all I want. I want to give *you* my name too."

I shook my head again, another tear escaping and slipping down my face.

He took another step closer. "Is that not what you want? Did you not mean what you said earlier when you said you loved me?"

"Of course I meant it," I spat out.

He smiled and I wanted to both smack it off his face and jump him at the same time. Damn infuriating man.

"We can be the family that neither of us ever had," he said. "I'll inherit my father's company. That's why I had to stay there and accept their robe and go through all that bullshit. I couldn't jeopardize the future and stability I'll need for you and our son. It was more important than ever. But it killed me to see you leave that room and not follow you."

I couldn't hold myself back from him any longer. I threw my arms around his neck.

He sighed in relief. "There she is."

I clung to him and for the first time, I actually believed it. Oh God, I believed it.

He loved me. He wanted *me*. There was no Order *forcing* him to accept my equal claim on this child, no money giving me equal power. He was choosing me freely. Choosing a life with me, choosing to be father to our son. Choosing to be a good man. Because it was simply who he was.

I buried my face in his neck and clung to him. "I love you so much," I said.

"Good," he said, pulling back from me. "Because I want to give you everything. Starting with this."

I frowned in confusion, but then he pulled something out of his pocket. Something with diamonds and gemstones that glinted in the Georgian summer sun.

It was a necklace with a huge pendant.

I gasped. I couldn't help it.

"The Order might not have given you all the money you wanted, but you'll be a Radcliffe one day, and as such, here is just a token of all that will be yours."

I froze as he lifted my hair and clasped the heavy pendant around my neck.

"Beau, what are you doing?" I whispered, my fingers fluttering as I lifted them to touch the pendant, stopping at the last second. I couldn't imagine getting even a single smudge from my fingers on the exquisite setting.

"Marking you as mine, naturally." He grinned wickedly as he stepped back from me. The pendant hung heavy around my neck. "And giving you your due reward for passing the Trials with flying colors. That pendant is worth a million dollars. So now you can feel that at least you're on a little bit more of an equal playing field when it comes to our son. I know that was important to you, and I want that for you."

I threw my arms around him and kissed him hard as the sunshine twinkled down on us through the swaying oak trees. Beau holding me so tight, loving me, our baby between us growing in my tummy.

A lifetime of dreams come true.

EPILOGUE
BELLAMY CARMICHAEL

I sat with my mother waiting for the wedding that the entire Darlington County social calendar had been aflutter about.

Montgomery Kingston was getting married. He was the first of the counties' most eligible young bachelors to tie the knot, and everybody who was anybody was here.

"Can you believe the scandal?" my mother leaned over and whispered in my ear. "You know she's one of the belles from that silly secret society of theirs."

I nodded, rolling my eyes. "You've only told me about fifteen times," I whispered back.

"Well, just look at them. It's happening to all of them. Six of the most eligible bachelors in this county and four of them are with trash from the wrong side of the tracks because of that mess. That's not the way it was done back in my day. They dallied with the whores, but then they *married* from respectable stock."

"Jesus, Mom." I glared at her, but she just glared right back.

"Don't you take the Lord's name in vain with me. I raised you to be a *lady*."

I tried not to snort at that. A *lady*. What was this, the eighteen hundreds? But it was true. My mother had done her best to raise a Southern belle. I'd even gone to cotillion for Christ's sake. The groom himself, Montgomery Kingston, had been my cotillion partner.

My mother had naturally cooed about how perfect we were for one another and had schemed about us getting married one day.

I was fourteen. Montgomery was fifteen. He'd been bored out of his mind by the whole thing and barely looked at me. Understandable, but even then, it messed with my head, my mom constantly talking about my *marriage prospects* like I was in a Jane Austen novel.

I'd grown up with the boys at Darlington Prep and occasionally gone out with one or another of them. But I'd been brought up to be such a proper *lady* that whenever they wanted to go make out under the bleachers, I always demurred, saying I couldn't possibly. Not shockingly, I was regularly broken up with after a few months.

Because another thing about proper ladyhood? It meant I didn't know how to talk to guys. I knew people thought I was a stuck-up snob. That was the reputation I'd gained around Darlington Prep anyway. Really, I was just shy.

But if being from one of the oldest and most respected families in Darlington plus being shy inevitably was interpreted as snobbishness, fine. I eventually just leaned into it. It meant I didn't have to try to attempt awkward conversations. I could be aloof and shy, and people just let me do it without question. So what if behind my back they called me a snobbish bitch?

Eventually, I stopped trying the awkward relationships with the boys around me. Which earned me the title Ice Princess. Apparently, I thought I was too good for the boys of Darlington. Or I was secretly dating college boys. Rumors abounded, as rumors tended to do.

The truth?

Mom and Dad's marriage was falling apart. The family money was all gone. All we had left was a name, which Mom clung to as if it was life itself. She still paraded around town in designer wear that was a decade out of style as our bills piled up.

After high school, there was no money for me to go to college, at least not the kind of colleges my mother wanted for her daughter. But it wasn't like I could apply for scholarships, because that would have equally mortified her. Appearance was everything to the woman.

When Dad got sick, I just ended up staying home after school anyway to help take care of him. And the years passed.

Mom still presided as the Queen of Darlington because it was all she had left. And she protected the secret of our near bankruptcy with the ferocity of a dragon protecting a treasure. The thought of anyone knowing she was in diminished circumstances was her worst fear.

So here we were, all dolled up, in the second row with Darlington's best and brightest, attending the wedding of the year.

Mom suddenly reached out and grasped my hand. "You have to do it. I can get you an invitation. It's the only way."

I frowned and tried to pull free of her claw-like grip on my hand. "What are you talking about?" I hissed.

Her nails dug into my wrist, though. There was no getting free.

"It's perfect, don't you see? I can get you an invitation so you can be one of those harlot belles. Then you can entice one of those two boys who are left with your charms. You can get them to marry you and save the family!"

My mouth must have dropped open because she snapped at me, "Close your mouth, you look like a fish. It's unattractive. And let's be honest, all you have are your looks at this point. It's time to grow up and face facts. You think your father fell in love with me because of my intellect? No. Men respond to a pretty face and thank the Lord you aren't too old yet. Though don't think I haven't noticed those lines around your eyes. It's the first sign of aging."

"Jesus, Mom, I'm only twenty-four!"

"Don't take the Lord's name in vain. No man wants a lady who's uncouth."

I looked away from my mother and glared at the perfectly manicured grass underneath us. Because that was always what it came down to for my mother, wasn't it? What a *man* wanted. How I looked to a *man*. That had always been my only worth. My mother had never talked about what career I might grow up to have. She'd never encouraged any interest beyond my looks and critiquing my weight or make-up.

I thought about the little she'd spoken of in regard to the secret society the men in town were part of. Usually she spoke about it in disgusted tones, which was why it was absolutely *rich* that she was now willing to throw me under the bus if it meant she could get me married off at the end of it. There were orgies, for Christ's sake. Orgies and like, demonic rituals, if the rumors were to be believed. Crazy, freaky shit.

But then, the rumors about me had always been exaggerated, so surely these were too.

I looked up to the front where Montgomery stood, smiling widely as he waited for his bride. Five men flanked him, his best men.

"Who would it be?" I suddenly asked, flushed with a wild curiosity and recklessness.

My mother pounced on the opportunity. "The one closest to Montgomery, that's Walker. And the one on the end. Emmett."

The fact that she was so ready to point them out had me thinking that this wasn't just a spur of the moment suggestion. How long had she been thinking about springing this one on me?

I tamped down my fury at her and looked at the two men. I knew both of them a little from my time at Darlington, at least in passing. They'd been in the grade ahead of me, but everyone had idolized the group of friends. Walker especially had been a big personality on campus. He and Montgomery were two of the biggest legacy kids in Darlington. That kind of swagger had always been a turn off to me.

I turned my sights to the man standing at the end. Emmett. I didn't remember so much about him. But he was tall and broad-shouldered and so handsome I had to shift in my seat just from watching him.

"Emmett," I said to my mother. "Get me an Invitation for his Trial."

Her face lit up so much it was like I'd announced Christmas in July. "Done."

Oh, Mother, Mother. She had no idea, but I had no intention of playing along with her games and schemes.

Yes, I would go and see what the secret society was all about. If there were orgies, I would participate in orgies. I would throw off being a *good girl* once and for all in spectacular fashion.

But there was no way in *hell* I would come out married at the end of it. I was done living according to how everybody else, including my mother, thought I should be.

The bridal march started, and both my mom and I stood. The grinning bride, stars in her eyes, started down the aisle toward Montgomery.

And for the first time in a long time, I felt excited about my own future too.

———

Don't stop reading yet.
The Breaking Belles series continues with the next book in the series
Delicate Revenge (https://geni.us/DeRe-EN-n)
Are you ready for Emmett and Bellamy's story?

———

Want a **bonus scene** of a dark initiation ritual between Grace and Montgomery, the main characters from Elegant Sins? For some extra dark, extra sacrilegious sizzle, read the scene that was too dark to make it into the book.
Go to BookHip.com/WPQXMJ to get it NOW!

ALSO BY STASIA BLACK

DARK CONTEMPORARY ROMANCES

BREAKING BELLES SERIES

Elegant Sins [https://geni.us/ElSi-EN-w]

Beautiful Lies [https://geni.us/BeLi-EN-w]

Opulent Obsession [https://geni.us/OpOb-EN-w]

Inherited Malice [https://geni.us/InMa-EN-w]

Delicate Revenge [https://geni.us/DeRe-EN-w]

Lavish Corruption

DARK MAFIA SERIES

Innocence [https://geni.us/Innocence-EN-w]

Awakening [https://geni.us/Awakening-EN-w]

Queen of the Underworld [https://geni.us/
QuOfThUn-EN-w]

The Innocence Trilogy [https://geni.us/InBx-EN-w]

BEAUTY AND THE ROSE SERIES

Beauty's Beast [https://geni.us/BeBe-EN-w]

Beauty and the Thorns [https://geni.us/BeNThTh-EN-w]

Beauty and the Rose [https://geni.us/BeNThRo-EN-w]

Billionaire's Captive [https://geni.us/BiCa-EN-w]

Love So Dark Duology

Cut So Deep [https://geni.us/CuSDe-EN-w]

Break So Soft [https://geni.us/BrSSo-EN-w]

Love So Dark [https://geni.us/LoSDa-EN-w]

Stud Ranch Series

The Virgin and the Beast [https://geni.us/ThViNThBe-EN-w]

Hunter [https://geni.us/Hunter-EN-w]

The Virgin Next Door [https://geni.us/ThViNeDo-EN-w]

Reece [https://geni.us/Reece-EN-w]

Jeremiah

Taboo Series

Daddy's Sweet Girl [https://geni.us/DaSwGi-EN-w]

Hurt So Good [https://geni.us/HuSGo-EN-w]

Taboo: a Dark Romance Boxset Collection [https://geni.us/Taboo_Bx-EN-w]

VASILIEV BRATVA SERIES

Without Remorse [https://geni.us/WiRe-EN-w]

FREEBIE

Indecent: A Taboo Proposal [https://geni.us/SBA-nw-cont-w]

SCI-FI ROMANCES

DRACI ALIEN SERIES

My Alien's Obsession [https://geni.us/MyAlOb-EN-w]

My Alien's Baby [https://geni.us/MyAlBa-EN-w]

My Alien's Beast [https://geni.us/MyAlBe-EN-w]

MARRIAGE RAFFLE SERIES

Theirs To Protect [https://geni.us/Th2Pr-EN-w]

Theirs To Pleasure [https://geni.us/Th2Pl-EN-w]

Theirs To Wed [https://geni.us/Th2We-EN-w]

Theirs To Defy [https://geni.us/Th2De-EN-w]

Theirs To Ransom [https://geni.us/Th2Ra-EN-w]

Marriage Raffle Boxset Part 1 [https://geni.us/MaRaBx-EN-w]

Marriage Raffle Boxset Part 2 [https://geni.us/MaRaBx-2-EN-w]

FREEBIE

Their Honeymoon [https://BookHip.com/QHCQDM]

ALSO BY ALTA HENSLEY

For all of my books, check out my Amazon Page!

http://amzn.to/2CTmeen

<u>Secret Bride Series:</u>

Captive Bride

Kept Bride

Taken Bride

<u>Top Shelf Series:</u>

Bastards & Whiskey

Villains & Vodka

Scoundrels & Scotch

Devils & Rye

Beasts & Bourbon

Sinners & Gin

Evil Lies Series:

The Truth About Cinder

The Truth About Alice

Breaking Belles Series:

Elegant Sins

Beautiful Lies

Opulent Obsession

Inherited Malice

Delicate Revenge

Lavish Corruption

Dark Fantasy Series:

Snow & the Seven Huntsmen

Red & the Wolves

Queen & the Kingsmen

Mr. D

ABOUT STASIA BLACK

STASIA BLACK grew up in Texas, recently spent a freezing five-year stint in Minnesota, and now is happily planted in sunny California, which she will never, ever leave.

She loves writing, reading, listening to podcasts, and has recently taken up biking after a twenty-year sabbatical (and has the bumps and bruises to prove it). She lives with her own personal cheerleader, aka, her handsome husband, and their teenage son. Wow. Typing that makes her feel old. And writing about herself in the third person makes her feel a little like a nutjob, but ahem! Where were we?

Stasia's drawn to romantic stories that don't take the easy way out. She wants to see beneath people's veneer and poke into their dark places, their twisted motives, and their deepest desires. Basically, she wants to create characters that make readers alternately laugh, cry ugly tears, want to toss their kindles across the room, and then declare they have a new FBB (forever book boyfriend).

Join Stasia's Facebook Group for Readers for access to deleted scenes, to chat with me and other fans and also get access to exclusive giveaways:

Stasia's Facebook Reader Group

(facebook.com/groups/1047415562052038/)

Want to read an EXCLUSIVE, FREE novella, Indecent: a Taboo Proposal, that is available ONLY to my newsletter subscribers, along with news about upcoming releases, sales, exclusive giveaways, and more?

Get **Indecent: a Taboo Proposal**

(geni.us/SBA-nw-cont-w)

When Mia's boyfriend takes her out to her favorite restaurant on their six-year anniversary, she's expecting one kind of proposal. What she didn't expect was her boyfriend's longtime rival, Vaughn

McBride, to show up and make a completely different sort of offer: all her boyfriend's debts will be wiped clear. The price?

One night with her.

ABOUT ALTA HENSLEY

Alta Hensley is a USA TODAY bestselling author of hot, dark and dirty romance. She is also an Amazon Top 100 bestselling author. Being a multi-published author in the romance genre, Alta is known for her dark, gritty alpha heroes, sometimes sweet love stories, hot eroticism, and engaging tales of the constant struggle between dominance and submission.

As a gift for being my reader, I would like to offer you a FREE book.

DELICATE SCARS

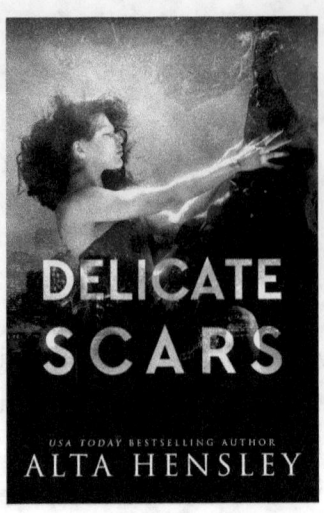

Get your copy now! ~

https://dl.bookfunnel.com/tnpuad5675

I was going to ruin her.

I knew it the moment I laid eyes on her. She was too naive, too innocent.

I would wrap her in the darkness of my world till she no longer craved the light... only me.

I should walk away, leave her clean and untouched... but I won't.

I hold her delicate heart in my scarred fist and I have no intention of letting go.

It all started with a book... doesn't that sound crazy?

For your entire world to come crashing down around you over research for a book?

But that is what it felt like the moment I met him.

My world tilted. Nothing made sense any more.

I only know he became like a drug to me... and I shook with need till my next fix.

Join Alta's Facebook Group for Readers for access to deleted scenes, to chat with me and other fans and also get access to exclusive giveaways:
Alta's Private Facebook Room

Check out Alta Hensley:
Website: www.altahensley.com
Facebook: facebook.com/AltaHensleyAuthor

Twitter: twitter.com/AltaHensley

Instagram: instagram.com/altahensley

BookBub: bookbub.com/authors/alta-hensley

Sign up for Alta's Newsletter: readerlinks.
com/l/727720/nl